Go far from home
and you will have
a long way back.

—An Amish Proverb

SUGARCREEK AMISH MYSTERIES

Quilt by Association

NANCY MEHL

Guideposts

New York

Sugarcreek Amish Mysteries is a trademark of Guideposts.

Published by Guideposts Books & Inspirational Media
110 William Street
New York, NY 10038
Guideposts.org

This is a work of fiction. Sugarcreek, Ohio, actually exists, and some characters
are based on actual residents whose identities have been fictionalized to protect their
privacy. All other names, characters, businesses, and events are the creation of the
author's imagination, and any resemblance to actual persons or events is coincidental.

Every attempt has been made to credit the sources of copyrighted material used in
this book. If any such acknowledgment has been inadvertently omitted or
miscredited, receipt of such information would be appreciated.

Scripture references are from the following sources: The Holy Bible, King James
Version (KJV). Scripture quotations marked (NIV) are taken from *The Holy Bible,
New International Version*. Copyright ©1973, 1978, 1984, 2011 by Biblica, Inc. Used
by permission of Zondervan. All rights reserved worldwide. www.zondervan.com

Cover and interior design by Müllerhaus
Cover illustration by Bill Bruning, represented by Deborah Wolfe, LTD.
Typeset by Aptara, Inc.

Printed and bound in the United States of America
10 9 8 7 6 5 4 3

Dedication

This book is dedicated to Nancy Edwards Darby,
a woman with many wonderful gifts. One of them
is the ability to craft gorgeous quilts, which she generously
gives to her friends. But even more importantly, she knows
how to fashion a truly beautiful life using threads of love,
joy, humor, bravery, and a genuine love of God.
I am one of the people blessed to be
touched by her incredible spirit.

I love you, Nancy.

CHAPTER ONE

Cheryl Miller looked out the window of the cottage where she'd lived when she first came to Sugarcreek. So many things had changed since then. A tug on the back of her jeans caused her to look down at her seventeen-month-old daughter, Rebecca.

"What is it, Boo Bear?" she asked.

Rebecca put her arms up. "Mama, Mama, Mama…" she repeated over and over.

Cheryl bent down to pick her up. She nuzzled Rebecca's neck, taking in the aroma of baby shampoo. "I love you," she said.

Rebecca squealed in happiness, but after a few moments of snuggling, she was ready to get down. She wriggled until Cheryl put her on the floor.

"Don't get into anything," Cheryl told her, as if Rebecca had the ability to control her curiosity.

Aunt Mitzi's cottage was comfortable and charming but different from when Cheryl lived there. Many of her aunt's personal possessions were now in Cheryl's house. Several people had rented the cottage since Cheryl moved out, but it was empty right now, so it worked out perfectly that an Amish woman from Bird-in-Hand, Pennsylvania was arriving soon to stay for the week. The woman, Sharon Vogel, was bringing some of her homemade quilts to sell in the Swiss Miss. Cheryl had invited her to Sugarcreek so they could talk and so that Cheryl and Esther, who was managing the store now, could see some of her quilts firsthand. Sharon's church had given her permission to ride a bus to Canton, Ohio, where Cheryl's husband, Levi, and his mother, Naomi, would pick her up and drive her to Sugarcreek.

Cheryl glanced at the clock. They were running a little late. Cheryl hoped everything was all right. She noticed Rebecca headed for some of Aunt Mitzi's knickknacks on a nearby desk. Keeping Rebecca out of things wasn't easy. She was getting pretty fast. Her little hands could pick up a glass or a cup before her parents had a chance to stop her. Cheryl ran toward the desk and grabbed her.

"Where's your dolly?" she asked. She steered Rebecca away from the desk, retrieved the diaper bag, and pulled out the Amish doll Naomi had made for her. A lot of people believed all Amish dolls were faceless, but it wasn't true. Many of them had features. Naomi had painted blue eyes on the doll's face and sewn on a red smiling mouth. Rebecca's face lit up, and she put her hands out. Cheryl breathed a sigh of relief. Rebecca would stay busy with Oma for a while. Cheryl thought it was funny that Rebecca named her doll after her grandmother. Truth be told, the doll did look a little bit like Naomi. As Rebecca sat down on the floor with her doll, Cheryl heard a noise from outside and went back to the window. Levi's truck was pulling into the driveway.

Cheryl scooped Rebecca up in her arms and hurried to the front door. She opened it and watched as Levi got out and went around to the passenger side of the truck. Rebecca started laughing and saying, "Dada! Dada!" She certainly was a daddy's girl. She absolutely adored Levi.

Levi helped Sharon out of the truck. Cheryl guessed her to be in her late twenties or early thirties. She was small and very attractive, with a wide smile. She reached up to adjust her prayer *kapp* after a gust of wind swept past her. It was September in Sugarcreek. One of Cheryl's favorite times of the year. The trees were burnished red and gold, but the wind that came with the fall weather could be rough.

Sharon stood to the side while Levi helped his mother out. When she saw Cheryl and Rebecca, Naomi waved and grinned at them. Once she'd smoothed her dress, she put her arm through Sharon's and led her toward the house. Levi went to the back of the truck to get Sharon's suitcases.

When Naomi reached them, she let go of Sharon and held her arms out for Rebecca, who was excited to see her oma. Cheryl put her in Naomi's arms and turned to Sharon.

"I'm so happy to meet you," she said. "Thank you for coming all this way."

"I am grateful you are willing to look at my quilts."

"As I told you, I saw pictures of a couple of them at a charity auction," Cheryl said. "They were so beautiful. Very distinctive. I love the way you incorporate different fabrics into your designs. They're breathtaking. I'd really like to share them with my customers."

Sharon stepped up onto the porch. "I brought three quilts to show you. I'm looking forward to working with you and Esther."

"I am too." Cheryl held the door to the cottage open. "I believe you'll be comfortable here. As I told you, it does have electricity."

Sharon smiled. "Our bishop isn't as strict as some. When we travel or do business, we must accept different circumstances. I am grateful to have such a nice place to stay."

"I told Sharon she was welcome to stay with us," Naomi said, "but that the cottage is so much closer to the store."

"We just want you to be comfortable," Cheryl said.

"I am certain I will be just fine."

Cheryl noticed Levi coming up the walk with three suitcases balanced in his arms. She hurried over and opened the door. He carried the suitcases inside.

"Where do you want these, Sharon?" he asked.

"Perhaps in the bedroom?" she said. "I can unpack them later."

Levi nodded and headed toward the master bedroom.

"Unless you're tired, Sharon, we thought you might like to go by the shop and then come to our house for lunch," Cheryl said. "Naomi has done the cooking, so you're in for a treat."

"Thank you," Sharon said. "That would be wonderful. And perhaps afterwards on the way back we could stop by a grocery store? I would like to put some food in the house."

"We certainly can," Cheryl said, "but I've already stocked some things I thought you would like. You might want to check out the kitchen first. And I'd love for you to join us for meals while you're here."

Cheryl showed Sharon what was in the refrigerator and on the shelves.

"This is wonderful," Sharon said. "If it is all right, I would like to buy some oatmeal, some orange juice, and a bottle of chocolate syrup." She blushed. "I must confess that I like a cup of hot chocolate before going to sleep."

Naomi laughed. "I like hot chocolate too, Sharon. We are alike, ain't so?"

Sharon laughed too. "It seems we are." She looked at Cheryl. "I can see I will not need anything else. You are very thoughtful."

"We're just happy you're here. Do you need to freshen up before we leave?"

"If you do not mind, I would like that."

Cheryl showed her to the bathroom and then went back into the living room where her husband and mother-in-law waited. "She's very nice," she said. She started to ask them about their trip when her cell phone rang. She took the phone out of her pocket and said, "Hello?"

"It's Chief Twitchell. Uh . . . I need to talk to you. It's important. Can you come by the station?"

Cheryl hesitated. What was this about? "Well, I have a guest from out of town. We're headed over to the shop. Would it be possible to talk to you there?"

There was a long silence, and then Cheryl heard the chief cover the receiver so she couldn't hear what he was saying to someone else. A surge of concern rushed through her. Was something wrong?

Finally, he said, "That would be fine. Will Levi be with you?"

"Yes, he will."

"Good. We'll be there in a few minutes. We'll need to talk to the both of you in private."

"Chief, what's going on? Is everyone okay? Anyone hurt or sick?"

"Everyone is fine as far as I know. This is something different. Let's just talk when I see you."

"It sounds serious," Cheryl said.

He paused again. "It is," he said. "We'll explain when we see you." With that, he hung up.

Levi must have noticed her expression. "What's wrong?" he asked.

"I don't know. Chief Twitchell wants to talk to us. He says it's serious. He's meeting us at the shop. And he's bringing someone else." She frowned at her husband. "Do you have any idea what this is about?"

Levi shook his head. "Not a clue. I guess we will find out when we get there."

"I hope everything is all right," Sharon said. "Perhaps you would rather I wait here?"

Cheryl shook her head. "No. Let's keep our plans intact. It's probably nothing." But even as she tried to reassure Sharon, she felt strongly that her comment probably wasn't accurate.

Rebecca began to fuss for her mama, so Naomi held her out for Cheryl to take.

"I am certain it will be okay," Naomi said. "We must not assume the worst."

Cheryl nodded at her mother-in-law. "You're right," she said, but she noticed Naomi's pensive expression.

As they prepared to leave for the Swiss Miss, Cheryl couldn't help but worry. She tried to dismiss the fear that attempted to invade her thoughts, but something told her that unless it was very important, the chief wouldn't have approached them this way. What in the world could it be?

Chapter Two

When they arrived at the Swiss Miss, Cheryl could tell Sharon was impressed by the store with its turret room and charming details. Painted a cream color with cornflower-blue accents and red shutters, it looked a lot like the cottage. Cheryl smiled to herself. She was proud of the gift store. Over the last few years, she'd put a lot of effort into the shop. Business was brisk, and Cheryl was pleased with the quality they offered. There were other shops in town that catered to cheap, fake Amish gifts and food. But at the Swiss Miss, all the Amish gifts were made by people Cheryl knew, and they were all authentic.

"*Ach*, it smells so good in here," Sharon said when they stepped inside.

The aroma of cheeses and candles blended to create a pleasing ambiance. Cheryl never grew tired of it.

Esther, Naomi's daughter, saw them and hurried over. Lately Cheryl had been staying home with Rebecca while Esther ran the store. Cheryl came in when she could, but she never worried about the Swiss Miss. Despite some problems last month, Esther was now back to doing her typical wonderful work again, and Cheryl felt blessed to have someone like her who cared about the Swiss Miss just as much as she did.

"Sharon, this is Esther Miller," Cheryl said. "She manages the store."

"I am so happy to meet you," Esther said. "I saw pictures of your lovely quilts. Have you brought some with you?"

As if on cue, Levi pushed the front door open, a large box in his hands. "Where do you want this?" he asked Cheryl.

"Can you put it on the counter?"

Levi set the box down where Cheryl indicated.

Cheryl noticed Joni Blanchard, a young girl whose family had just moved to town, helping a customer who was interested in a colorful apron made by a local woman. Joni had made friends with Esther, who had recommended her to Cheryl.

"How is Joni doing?" she asked Esther in a low voice.

They'd hired her to help out part-time now and also to provide some assistance during the upcoming Swiss Festival. It was a busy time, when visitors flooded Sugarcreek.

"Very well," Esther answered. "She learns quickly, and the customers seem to like her."

Even though she was sixteen, Joni looked younger. Cheryl had met her mother briefly but not her father, who had transferred to Sugarcreek to work in one of the local banks. She was certainly impressed with how responsible Joni seemed to be.

Cheryl turned her attention to Sharon's quilts. She took the top off the box and looked inside. The pictures she'd seen didn't do justice to the real thing. Looking at them up close confirmed how special they were. Cheryl ran her hand over the top quilt, a patchwork of varying shades of blues and purples. It was breathtaking. The tiny, perfect stitches made it clear Sharon was a talented perfectionist. Cheryl took the quilt out of the box and put it on the counter. Underneath was a child's quilt. Cheryl couldn't hold back a gasp. It was smaller than the other quilt but absolutely stunning. It had a dark blue border with colorful squares against a white background. Cheryl removed it from the box and put it on top of the other quilt. She was just looking at the third quilt, which had a colorful star pattern, when the bell over the front door rang and Sam Twitchell, the village's police chief, entered. The pastor of Friendship Mennonite Church, where Cheryl and Levi attended, followed close behind him. Cheryl felt her stomach tighten. What was this about?

"Good morning, Levi, Esther, Cheryl," Pastor Lory said. "Levi, can the chief and I talk to you and Cheryl for a few minutes?"

"Of course," Levi said.

"We can go to my office." Cheryl turned to Sharon. "I'm sorry to leave you alone for a little bit." She smiled at Esther. "Can you show Sharon around the store? I'm sure she'd enjoy seeing all the different kinds of homemade gifts we have. And have her pick out a dessert to take back to the house."

Sharon started to protest, but Cheryl waved her comments away. "I want you to have something sweet to enjoy." She grinned. "I like to end my evening with something special. Maybe you'll want to do that too."

"I can eat it with my hot chocolate," Sharon said, smiling. "*Danki.*"

As Esther began to guide Sharon through the shop, Cheryl gestured to Levi, the chief, and Pastor Lory to follow her into the small office located behind the counter. Before they headed toward the office door, Naomi took Cheryl's arm.

"I will watch Rebecca while you talk to the chief. You and Levi do not need distractions."

Cheryl gave Naomi a quick hug. "Thank you so much. I know she'd love spending time with her oma."

"Her oma loves being with her too. You go on and do not worry about this little *liebling*."

Cheryl was grateful for Naomi's help and would probably lean on her even more during the festival. "Thank you," Cheryl said. She smiled as her mother-in-law and best friend snuggled with Rebecca. Dealing with her Amish son marrying an Englisher had been tough, but Cheryl and Naomi's close friendship had helped them navigate the troubled waters. Now, Naomi was thrilled to have Cheryl as her daughter, friend, and business partner. Cheryl's store sold more of Naomi's goods than anyone else in the village did. She also loved being a grandmother, and Rebecca adored her.

Cheryl leaned close to Naomi. "I'll tell you what the chief and Pastor Lory said later. Pray for us, okay?"

"I pray for you all the time," Naomi said. "And I am praying now, daughter."

"I know you do," Cheryl said gently.

"Let's go, Cheryl," Levi said. "The chief and Pastor Lory are waiting."

Cheryl followed Levi into her office. Chief Twitchell and Pastor Lory were seated in the chairs in front of Cheryl's desk.

Cheryl sat down in her desk chair and Levi stood behind her, his hand on her shoulder.

"What is it you want to talk to us about?" she asked the two men. Their dour expressions worried her.

The men exchanged a quick look. Pastor Lory cleared his throat. "We want to ask you for a favor," he said, "but it's something you may not want to do."

"I cannot think of anything we would not be willing to do if you asked," Levi said with a frown. "What about this request concerns you?"

"Do you remember Anton Birken?" Pastor Lory said.

Cheryl felt Levi's hand tense.

"*Ja*, of course I do," he said.

"Who is Anton Birken?" Cheryl said. She didn't remember hearing the name before.

"He was a young man in our community," Levi said, his voice grim. "He was friends with a girl named Liesel Hostettler. Then one day she disappeared. Anton was suspected of having something to do with it."

Cheryl turned her head to look up at her husband. "What do you mean she…disappeared?"

"He means just what he said," Chief Twitchell said. "We looked everywhere. Never found a trace of her. Her family is convinced that Anton did her harm."

Cheryl's mouth dropped open. "You mean…You mean…"

"They believe Anton took her life," Pastor Lory said. He leaned forward in his chair and put his hands on the edge of Cheryl's desk. "I never believed a word of it. I knew Anton. He was a little rebellious, yes, but not someone who would hurt another human being. You see, his father died when he was young. His mother, Ada, raised him and his sister, Meredith. Ada was brought up by very strict Amish parents. I'm afraid they cared more for rules than for understanding the purpose behind them. The Amish have very firm beliefs, but they're based on what they think is the best way to raise their families. The safest way."

"This is true," Levi said. "But there is love behind everything that is taught."

"But you know that doesn't always happen, Levi," Pastor Lory said.

Cheryl had seen it too, but not only in Amish families. In any family where God was seen as a harsh judge, without love or forgiveness.

"So that was the case with Anton?" Cheryl said.

Pastor Lory nodded. "We talked many times. He was troubled, but I am convinced he had nothing to do with Liesel Hostettler's disappearance."

"This is all very interesting," Cheryl said. "But what does it have to do with us?"

"You may have heard that Anton's mother just died," Chief Twitchell said.

Cheryl shook her head, but Levi said from behind her, "Ja, I have."

"Anton wants to attend the funeral. He hopes to bridge the divide between him and his sister."

"I have to ask again, what does this have to do with us?"

The chief and Pastor Lory looked at each other as if urging the other one to answer Cheryl's question. Finally, it seemed the chief won.

Pastor Lory met Cheryl's gaze. "We know you have a guest staying in your cottage. We want to ask you if Anton can live in your *dawdy haus* while he's in town."

Chapter Three

Cheryl and Levi were quiet for a few moments. Cheryl had no idea what her husband was thinking, but the idea of having someone accused of hurting a young girl actually staying so close to their house...It didn't sound safe, and Cheryl was certain Levi would say no.

"Pastor Lory and I are both absolutely convinced Anton had nothin' to do with what happened to Liesel," Chief Twitchell said. "I feel sorry for him. Family and friends deserted him, and now his mother has died. His sister says she has no desire to see him. I don't think his plan to make things right with her will turn out well."

"Not just because of what happened to Liesel," Pastor Lory said. "His sister blames Anton for breaking their mother's heart. When he left town, it really upset her. Meredith thinks it led to her death."

"After ten years?" Cheryl said. "That's not a very reasonable argument."

"I agree," Pastor Lory said. He sighed. "We've tried to find another place for Anton to stay, but we haven't been able to. With the festival coming up so soon, people who normally would have welcomed him into their homes can't do it because of company coming to town. We have relatives who plan to stay with us, or I'd put him in our spare bedroom. All the hotels, motels, and B&Bs are booked. Your dawdy haus was the only place we could come up with."

"What about the church?" Levi asked. "Couldn't you put him up there?"

"Maybe at some point, but the teenagers have a retreat planned the next two weekends. They'll be staying there nights, and during the week they'll be working every afternoon to get things ready." Pastor Lory shifted uncomfortably in his chair. "I'm afraid the parents in our church wouldn't appreciate it if I allowed him to stay in the building while their children were there." He cleared his throat. "He could probably find a place to stay in Canton, but I think he wants to spend time in Sugarcreek. He's been away a long time. Anton seemed to feel you'd put him up, Levi. I think you used to be friends?"

"Ja, we were," Levi said. "But that was a long time ago."

Obviously, Levi didn't feel compelled to offer Anton a place to stay. Pastor Lory would surely understand when they turned down his request. Before she had a chance to say anything, Levi spoke up.

"The roof of the dawdy haus began leaking after the hailstorm that came through here a couple of weeks ago. I need to replace it. We put our guest in the cottage because the dawdy haus was not in shape for a visitor."

Relief washed through Cheryl. Thank goodness for that leaky old roof. This way they could say no without sounding as if they were turning their backs on Mr. Birken.

"I did temporarily patch it," Levi continued. "I suppose it could hold up for a few days, but I will have to check it. Maybe reinforce the patches."

Shocked, Cheryl looked up at him, hoping she'd misheard.

"It won't take me long to make the improvements," he said. "When did you say Anton will arrive in town?"

Cheryl felt as if someone had thrown ice water on her head. Why would Levi agree to the pastor's request without talking to her first? It was true that he had been raised in an atmosphere where the husband made all the major decisions, and Cheryl accepted that the husband was the head of the household. Nevertheless, she and Levi decided before they were married that they would try to agree on important issues. Levi would make the final decision only when they couldn't see eye to eye.

She wanted to speak up, voice her opinion, but she decided to wait until she and Levi were alone. He was usually so protective of her and Rebecca. Why would he agree to this arrangement?

"Thank you, Levi," Pastor Lory said with a big smile. He stood up and stuck his hand out over the desk. Levi leaned over Cheryl and shook it.

"Anton will arrive here tomorrow," Chief Twitchell said. "He's been livin' in Colorado. Runs a real estate agency. Seems to do pretty well."

"And when will the funeral take place?" Levi asked.

"It's scheduled for Friday," Pastor Lory said. "At Meredith Kirchner's house. I doubt that she'll be happy to see Anton there."

"That is distressing," Levi said.

Pastor Lory sighed. "I'm sure he won't be put out. The Amish are mannerly above all. Peace must be maintained."

Cheryl knew the pastor's words were true. Shunning was rare nowadays. It hadn't happened for years at the church Naomi and her family attended. Even though Anton had left the church, he would still be welcome at his mother's funeral. His sister would have to find a way to deal with it.

Chief Twitchell stood up. "I hope you know that if I thought you were in any danger at all, Cheryl, we wouldn't ask you to help Anton. I investigated Liesel's disappearance ten years ago, and I was convinced Anton wasn't involved. Unfortunately, there was a group of men in his church who were sure he harmed the girl. Nothin' I said or did could change their minds. To this day, some of the members of that church don't trust me—or the police department."

"My family trusts you, Chief," Levi said.

"Thank you, Levi," the chief said. His hangdog expression lightened. The chief had a long nose and a narrow face. He wasn't a handsome man, but when he smiled his looks improved immensely. Cheryl was quite fond of him, and she respected his opinion. If he was convinced Anton Birken wasn't a problem, she wanted to believe him. Still, Anton's story bothered her.

"So Liesel was never found?" she said. "And she's been missing for ten years?"

The chief nodded. "I suspect she ran off. Wanted a different kind of life. Her parents loved her, but they were entrenched in the church and not willin' to let their daughter leave. They wouldn't even allow her to participate in *rumspringa*."

"But how could she just disappear like that?" Cheryl asked.

The chief shrugged. "It's done all the time. Sometimes people are found. Sometimes they're not. It was hard to believe Liesel wouldn't have let her parents know if she decided to run away. They were close. I think that's one reason so many people believe somethin' happened to her. I've looked for her down through the years, but I've never found even a trace of her."

Cheryl hoped the chief was right, and that the girl...now a woman...was safe and living under another name. It was certainly better than the alternative.

"Why were some people so sure Anton had something to do with what happened?" she asked.

"There was a note," the chief said. "'Meet me at the Noffsinger house tonight' it said. And it was signed *A*. But it was typed on a computer, and of course, Anton didn't have a computer."

"But he did spend time at the library," Pastor Lory said. "So according to some, he could have used the computer there. He was seen on it from time to time, even though he wasn't supposed to be using it."

"Liesel's parents found the note in her room after she went missin'," the chief said. "They were convinced Anton sent it. However, there wasn't any way to tie the note to him—or anyone else. Kinda convenient in my book. If Anton sent it, why didn't he just write it? That part always bothered me."

"Anton should arrive in town tomorrow some time after two o'clock," Pastor Lory said. "Thank you again for your compassion and generosity."

Cheryl followed the chief, Pastor Lory, and Levi out of the office. She found Sharon and Esther looking at the quilts Sharon had brought with her.

When Esther saw Cheryl, she smiled and her face lit up. "Ach, Cheryl. These quilts are so beautiful, ain't so? I am so happy we will be offering them in our shop."

Cheryl had shown Esther pictures of some of Sharon's quilts from a Mennonite relief sale near Sharon's home in Bird-in-Hand. Usually, the Swiss Miss only featured quilts from local quilt makers. But Sharon's work was so special, so unique, they'd decided to reach out and see if they could work out something with her. It had taken a while for Sharon to get permission from her bishop to travel alone to Sugarcreek and to stay in the cottage, which had electricity, but he had finally given her his blessing. It suddenly occurred to Cheryl that maybe Anton should stay in the cottage, and Sharon could take the dawdy haus. But Sharon had seemed so happy with the cottage, Cheryl hesitated to ask her to switch. She'd bring her idea up to Levi when she could get him alone. Cheryl would feel a lot better having Sharon close by and Anton farther away.

"They really are gorgeous," Cheryl said, running her hand over the quilt on top. Cheryl had already decided to buy it for herself. She wouldn't say anything to Sharon though. She didn't want Sharon to offer her a discount because she owned the store where the quilts were being offered. The Amish were very generous, giving people, and Cheryl learned a long time ago not to say she admired something to any Amish person. It might end up belonging to her before she finished her last syllable.

"I am grateful you like my work," Sharon said. "I am not married, and I have a lot of time on my hands. I needed to find something to do. My *maam* taught me to quilt. It has been such a blessing in my life. I meet with a group of friends every week. We quilt together." She smiled at Cheryl. "They will be waiting for my stories when I return to Bird-in-Hand. I can hardly wait to tell them about the beautiful cottage where you are allowing me to stay. I am truly blessed."

Cheryl's heart dropped. There was no way she could ask Sharon to stay in the dawdy haus now. It was nice, but it certainly didn't compare to the charm and coziness of the cottage.

Cheryl smiled. It wasn't Sharon's fault that Cheryl was facing the situation with Anton. She looked over at Levi who was trying to make Rebecca laugh as she sat on her oma's lap.

She trusted her husband and knew he always put his family first. So why was he insisting that someone like Anton Birken be housed so close to his wife and daughter?

She prayed he wasn't making a terrible mistake.

CHAPTER FOUR

After unpacking Sharon's quilts and finalizing an arrangement to purchase several more, Cheryl and Levi took Sharon over to their house. Naomi had dropped off some food early that morning, since she knew Cheryl would be busy. All she had to do was heat it up. As always, it was delicious. Cheryl had asked Naomi to eat with them, but she declined. Instead, she invited them over to her house for supper.

When lunch was over Cheryl noticed Sharon looked a little tired and offered to drive her back to the cottage to rest from her trip. Cheryl planned to go by the grocery store the next day and told Sharon she'd pick up the additional items she'd requested. Sharon seemed relieved. For a woman who lived a quiet life with her mother, this had probably been a very eventful day. Not to mention it had started in the wee hours of the morning with a bus ride from Pennsylvania.

After dropping Sharon off, they headed home. Rebecca loved riding in the truck and oohed and aahed every time she saw someone walking a dog. She also waved at everyone she saw. Cheryl and Levi had tried to stop her from being so friendly with strangers but had finally decided it wasn't right to suppress her affable spirit.

Cheryl was quiet as Levi drove. She was trying to figure out a way to tell him how she felt about Anton Birken without making it seem as if she didn't trust his decision. Finally, he said, "Is everything all right, Cheryl?"

She searched for the right words. Words that weren't angry. "You really think it's okay to house this...this Anton person so close to us? How can you be sure Rebecca and I will be safe?" She glanced over at him. "I wish you had talked to me before deciding to do this."

Levi took a deep breath and let it out slowly. "You might be right. I'd hoped you trusted me enough to believe I would never put my wife and daughter at risk."

"But Levi, how can we know for certain this guy isn't dangerous?" She noticed his knuckles were white as he gripped the steering wheel. What was going on? Why was this so personal to him? Realization dawned. "You were close to him, weren't you?"

He nodded. "We were friends, Cheryl. I know him very well. We grew up together and spent a lot of time together. I am certain he did not hurt Liesel. I believe she ran away and allowed Anton to suffer persecution."

"But why would she do that?"

"I do not know. Anton always said they were only friends. But maybe she wanted more and was angry that he did not return her feelings."

"So she ran away from her home and her parents because her pride was hurt? That doesn't sound right, Levi."

"Maybe not. I honestly do not know why she left. I only know that when she went missing, Anton told people the truth and they would not believe him. Even his family turned their backs on him. Anton was always a little rebellious. He should not have been meeting Liesel alone against her parents' wishes, but he was not a bad person."

"But I'm sure you defended him..." Cheryl stopped. "Oh, Levi. You didn't, did you? That's what this is about. And why you never told me about this. You're ashamed."

The muscles in his jaw tightened. "I tried to, but when people came against me...A bishop in our church at the time warned me that I could face expulsion if I took Anton's side in the matter. Instead of being brave, I backed down."

"Did you tell your parents?"

"Yes," Levi said. "My *daed* always believed Anton was innocent. He liked Anton and tried to be a father to him. He defended him. But the community would not listen. I wanted to back Daed up, but he told me to stay quiet. He did not want me to deal with the wrath of those who felt Anton had done something terrible to Liesel. Even my maam was not convinced of Anton's innocence." He sighed and glanced over at Cheryl. "Do not harshly judge my mother. Anton created most of his own problems. He got in trouble more than once. When he needed people to believe in him, the bad seed he had sown made it almost impossible for them to support him."

"But you..."

"I should have done more. My daed was only trying to protect me, but I should have been more mature. I was not the same person I am now." He gave her a small smile. "You have helped me to grow as a person, liebling. Today, I would not back down from being his friend. From telling others I trust him. So when I was asked to give him shelter..."

"You had a chance to do what you didn't do ten years ago."

"Ja. But I did not mean to make you feel insecure. I will withdraw my agreement if you want me to."

Cheryl reached over and put her hand on Levi's arm. "No. If you believe in him, I will too. It's time to heal this hurt in you. I'm with you."

Levi blinked several times and cleared his throat. It took him a few moments to whisper, "Thank you." He sighed. "I do not know how Anton will greet me. He has every reason to be angry with me."

Cheryl shrugged. "If he is, then he can turn down our offer. We'll just have to see what happens." She was glad now she hadn't said anything about putting Anton in the cottage. Sharon seemed happy, and Levi needed a chance to mend the broken bridge between him and his old friend. Having him close by should aid the process.

When they pulled up to the house, Cheryl got Rebecca out of her car seat while Levi held the truck door open. When Cheryl pulled Rebecca out, she stuck out her chubby little arms and said, "Dada, Dada, Dada, Dada!"

Cheryl laughed. "I guess you're the popular one today." She handed Rebecca to Levi, who smiled down at his daughter.

As they went inside, Cheryl noticed that the air had turned a little nippy. She loved fall in Sugarcreek, but this September was a little colder than normal. She was happy to feel the warmth inside their cozy home.

"I'll work on my grocery list," she told Levi as she took off her coat and Rebecca's.

"I need to check the roof of the dawdy haus," Levi said. "I'll have to take care of the well later. I know we don't let Rebecca run around unaccompanied, but it still worries me."

Levi had recently discovered an old well on their property. Someone had tried to cover it up, but the wooden boards they used had rotted out.

"How are you going to fix it?" Cheryl asked.

"As soon as I can I will cover it with plywood," he said, "but eventually we will have to have it sealed by a contractor who is approved by the state."

"How much will that cost?" Cheryl asked.

Levi shrugged. "I do not know, but it is the law so we will simply have to comply."

"Do you think plywood is enough for now?"

"Ja. The well is not near our crop fields, and is in a place no one should be walking. I believe it will be fine until we take proper care of it." He sighed. "Right now I need to focus on the dawdy haus. I believe the patches will hold, but since I did not plan on them remaining long, I want to make sure they will stay in place. I believe we are supposed to get storms by the end of the week. I need to make sure the patches will stay secure in bad weather. It should not take me long."

He placed Rebecca down on the floor, and Cheryl got out some of her toys. Hopefully, she'd sit and play for a while. Since Rebecca had started walking, chasing after her was almost a full-time job.

But for now she seemed content to stack the wooden building blocks her uncle Eli had made for her. Esther had painted pictures and numbers on them. Rebecca loved them.

Beau, the Millers' Siamese cat, was curled up on the back of the couch, lying in the sun that filtered through the window. Rebecca saw him and began calling, "Beau, Beau, Beau!"

Beau opened one eye and stared at her. Feeling safe from his perch, he closed his eye and went back to sleep. Although he was very good with Rebecca, sometimes he liked to avoid being picked up and carried around like a rag doll. Cheryl couldn't blame him. After trying several times to get his attention, Rebecca finally gave up and decided to focus on her toys.

After Levi left, Cheryl sat down at the kitchen table and started working on a list for the grocery store. She hoped Anton would join them for some meals. She decided she should also put some food and supplies in the dawdy haus before he arrived. Their last tenants had moved out and into their own home a couple of weeks earlier. Cheryl had cleaned the house after they left, but she wanted to check it out again. Make sure the house was spotless. When Levi got back, she'd ask him to watch Rebecca for a while so she could get things ready.

As she worked on her list, her thoughts ran to how she could help Levi heal the gap between him and Anton. And she worried a little bit about how others would feel about their decision to host him.

She assumed Levi would tell his family about his decision tonight over supper. Would the reaction be positive? What if it wasn't? Was Cheryl ready for the backlash they might receive from friends and family? She wasn't certain she was.

CHAPTER FIVE

That evening, after picking up Sharon, they headed for the Millers' farm. When they turned off the road and crossed the bridge to the large white farmhouse, Rebecca squealed with delight. She loved visiting Oma and *Opa*. Their dog, Rover, was waiting for them on the front porch. He ran out to the truck, barking with excitement. He was such a good dog, so gentle with Rebecca. She adored him. She also loved seeing the Millers' horses, but that visit would have to wait until after supper. She pointed at Samson, standing in the corral as they drove by. Methuselah and Obadiah looked on with interest as Levi parked the truck. The Millers' other two horses, Sugar and Spice, must have been out in the pasture.

Seth, Levi's father, walked out onto the front porch and then down the stairs. "Can I help?" he asked as he approached. Traveling with a toddler meant carrying a diaper bag, toys, and food just in case Rebecca wasn't interested in whatever Naomi had made for dinner. She usually wasn't too fussy, but she certainly had her likes and dislikes. Ever since Oma's sausage and sauerkraut, Rebecca had become somewhat suspicious of anything her grandmother put in front of her. Obviously, sauerkraut was not going to be on Rebecca's list of favorite foods.

Cheryl started to hand the diaper bag to Seth, but Rebecca laughed and held her arms out for her *opa*.

"I guess Rebecca has decided what you should carry," Cheryl said, grinning.

Seth reached out and took Rebecca from Cheryl's arms. "Now this is the very best package of all," he said, laughing.

Sharon got out and walked around the truck. Seth nodded at her.

"Seth, this is Sharon Vogel, the woman from Bird-in-Hand, Pennsylvania, I told you about. She's brought some of her beautiful quilts to town, and we'll be selling them in the store."

"I am pleased to meet you," Seth said. "We are blessed to have you in our home."

"I am happy to meet you too," Sharon said. "Thank you so much for inviting me."

Rover jumped up on Seth's overalls, trying to get to Rebecca. She laughed and tried to reach down to touch the excited dog.

"Doggy," she hollered. "Doggy, doggy, doggy!"

Seth sternly ordered Rover to get down. He obeyed, but reluctantly. Levi leaned down and stroked his head. "Be patient, my friend. You will be able to play with Rebecca after supper."

"Your maam has supper ready," Seth told Levi. "We should probably get inside before she begins to worry."

Cheryl smiled. Naomi was an incredible cook, but once the food was prepared, she liked to serve it while it was hot. With a large family, sometimes not everyone was ready at the same time. Naomi's consternation was a source of amusement to her children.

"Maam threatens to dump all the food out if we do not reach the table within a few minutes after she puts it on the table," Esther had told her once. "I am afraid my brothers sometimes dillydally just to evoke a reaction."

When they stepped inside the house, the aromas from the kitchen made Cheryl's mouth water. Naomi came out of the kitchen, her face red with exertion and her apron wrapped tightly around her waist.

"I am glad you are finally here," she said. "Please sit down before my food gets cold."

"Maam, we are a few minutes early," Levi said. "Why do you make it sound as if we are late?"

"You are supposed to magically know when the food is ready," Seth said under his breath. Then he smiled at his wife. "They are here now. We will sit down at the table."

Naomi sighed with relief and went back into the kitchen. Within a few minutes, everyone was seated around the huge table in the center of the kitchen. This was the real heart of the Miller house. The place where everyone gathered. The Miller children—Caleb, along with his young family, and Eli, and Elizabeth—were gathered around the table. Esther was closing up the Swiss Miss and would be a little late.

Naomi insisted that Rebecca's high chair be placed next to her. She loved feeding her granddaughter, and Cheryl was happy to let her do it. It gave her a break.

Everyone bowed his or her head in silent prayer. Levi had been brought up this way. Praying out loud before meals had been a challenge for him at first, but now he was fine with it. Little Rebecca had learned to bow her head when her daddy prayed. When he finished, she'd started clapping and saying "Yay!" At first, Levi was startled by her reaction, but in the end, he decided that cheering God was probably a good thing. Besides, Rebecca was so cute when she got excited about her daddy's prayer, there was no way they could tell her to stop.

When Seth lifted his head, the rest of the family lifted theirs. He began to pass the food around the table. Naomi had made her incredible pot roast with onions, potatoes, and carrots. Cheryl had tried cooking roast exactly the same way, but for some reason it wasn't ever as good as Naomi's. Levi didn't seem to mind. In fact, he always appeared to enjoy the food Cheryl made. She wasn't sure if it was love or if he just wasn't that picky.

"Naomi, the fried chicken you made for our lunch was absolutely delicious," Cheryl said. "I can't believe I get to eat two of your meals in one day."

Naomi blushed. "You stroke my ego, daughter. Shame on you," she said with a smile.

Seth laughed. "You love every word of it," he said. "And Cheryl is right. You are a wonderful cook. We are all blessed by your talent."

Naomi shushed him, but it was obvious she was pleased.

Levi took the time to introduce everyone at the table to Sharon, who seemed a little overwhelmed by the Millers. She told Cheryl that she'd grown up an only child, which was unusual in an Amish family. Her father died when she was young. After his death, it was just Sharon and her mother. It had been that way ever since. Sharon was twenty-seven years old and had never married, which was also unusual in the Amish community. At this point, she was considered an old maid. It didn't mean she would never marry, but it certainly limited her choices.

Although she was a little shy at first, before long, the Millers had put her at ease. She seemed to be enjoying herself.

About fifteen minutes into the meal, the front door opened and Esther came in. She greeted everyone and sat down at the table.

"I just put your quilts out," she told Sharon. "One sold immediately, and we have interest in another."

Cheryl smiled to herself. Esther didn't tell Sharon that the quilt that sold had gone to Cheryl. "I was hoping we'd have some available for the festival," Cheryl said. "They may not last that long."

"I am honored that people like them," Sharon said softly. "I have always given them away to friends and family. If I had not donated a couple to the Mennonite Charity Sale, you would never have seen them, Cheryl."

"Well, I'm glad one of my customers brought me a copy of the brochure. She was at the sale and was so impressed by your work. Looks like I'll be able to send some money home with you."

Sharon smiled. "It will be most welcome. Thank you." She hesitated a moment. "I do have some other quilts at home. I could ask my mother to send them if you wish."

"Oh, that would be great, Sharon," Cheryl said. "Please do. How many more do you have?"

"Well, I probably have six or seven, but there are three that I think would be appropriate for your store."

"Then have them sent. I would love to display them in the store during the festival."

Sharon put down her fork. "Maybe you could help me get a message to my mother? There is a woman who lives not far from us. We buy our eggs from her. She has a phone. If I could contact her, she could talk to my mother."

"Of course. Do you have the woman's number?"

Sharon nodded. "It is at the cottage. I will give it to you when you take me back. And I will describe the quilts I want."

"Sounds wonderful," Cheryl said. "I'm very excited to see more of your work."

Sharon's cheeks turned pink, and she smiled again. It seemed to Cheryl that she wasn't used to a lot of praise from anyone besides her mother.

Levi glanced at Cheryl and raised his eyebrows, a sign that he was getting ready to tell his family about Anton. For some reason she felt nervous. What would they say? Naomi was the most kindhearted person Cheryl had ever known. Surely, she would understand. And Seth had believed Anton was innocent. Hopefully, he still felt the same way.

Cheryl sighed. There was no way around it. They had to be told. She adopted the Amish way of praying and silently pleaded with God to help them keep peace in the family.

Chapter Six

A s Levi cleared his throat, Cheryl took a defensive stand by sticking a large piece of roasted potato in her mouth.

"Maam and Daed, do you remember Anton Birken?"

At Anton's name, Naomi gasped. Definitely not a good sign.

"Ja, I remember him," Seth said. "He was a good young man who made some mistakes, but he did not hurt that Hostettler girl. He was not treated right by the people in this village. It is shameful that he felt he had to leave town." He frowned at his son. "Why do you bring him up?"

Levi cleared his throat and looked at Naomi, who was staring at her son with an expression that only a mother could give. Cheryl recognized that look. Her own mother was an expert with it. Nothing struck fear into the heart of a child more than *the look*. And it worked no matter how old you were. Levi glanced at Cheryl as if wanting help. In response, she lifted her fork again and took another bite of potato. Then she shrugged. It was cowardly, but seemed necessary at the moment.

Levi scowled at her and turned his attention back to his father. "Pastor Lory and Chief Twitchell approached us earlier today. You know Anton's mother has passed away."

"Of course we know," Naomi said. "I am cooking for the funeral. She was a dear friend." Naomi sniffed. "Anton caused her a lot of pain. His sister has taken over the funeral arrangements by herself. She has suffered quite a bit as well from her brother's actions."

After chewing as long as humanly possible without looking as if she had some kind of physical malady, Cheryl finally spoke up.

"I wasn't here when the girl disappeared, but my understanding is that there was never any proof that Anton was involved," she said.

"Perhaps there was not the kind of *proof* you would like," Naomi said, "but Anton was trouble long before Liesel disappeared. Do you really think it was coincidence that a month after he began to chase after her, she vanished? I am afraid I cannot accept that as anything but *proof* he was involved."

Cheryl looked at her friend with her mouth open. Finally, she said, "Naomi, after everything we've been through, the times we've had to search for the truth, haven't you learned not to jump to conclusions?" Although her comment sounded a little harsh, Cheryl was flummoxed by Naomi's attitude. Usually, her mother-in-law gave everyone the benefit of the doubt. She was certainly not the kind of person Cheryl would call judgmental. Yet she had decided Anton was guilty without any direct evidence. How could that be?

Naomi straightened up in her chair. "You were not living in Sugarcreek back then. You do not know."

"You're right," Cheryl said. "But what if you're wrong? What if Anton's sister is wrong? Wouldn't that be awful?"

"I do not believe I am wrong." Naomi's statement sounded convincing, but Cheryl knew her well enough to hear some hesitation in her voice. She doubted, however, it would be enough to keep Naomi calm when Levi told them about Anton's visit to Sugarcreek. She looked over at him, but he wouldn't meet her eyes. Had he chickened out? She coughed lightly, trying to get his attention. Finally, he met her gaze.

"Maam and Daed," he said slowly, "Chief Twitchell and Pastor Lory have asked us to allow Anton to stay in the dawdy haus for a few days. He is coming for the funeral."

Naomi's mouth dropped open.

"Do you think this is wise?" Esther asked. "You will not be at home all the time, Levi. Cheryl and Rebecca will be alone."

"I have thought about that," Levi said. "I have decided to take Anton with me whenever I have to leave. I do not want to offend him, but I believe for everyone's peace of mind and to calm people's fears, this would be the best course to follow."

Cheryl felt a strong sense of relief from Levi's words. She'd had a hard time believing that he would leave her and Rebecca unprotected, no matter how much he believed in Anton's innocence. Of course, he had a plan. She should have known.

Seth nodded slowly. "I am not sure this is a good idea, Son, but if you feel you must do it, I am glad you will take precautions. Even though I believe in Anton's innocence, with family we must never take chances."

Levi glanced around the table. "I did not believe Anton was guilty when this occurred, and I still feel the same way. There are many reasons for people to go missing. We have seen it here, in Sugarcreek. More than once."

"We have experienced the same thing in Lancaster County," Sharon said hesitantly. "Sometimes young people leave the community because they do not want to live the Amish lifestyle." She frowned. "Usually, they contact their parents to let them know they are safe, but I had a friend who ran away when we were younger. I never heard from her again."

"As my husband said, we have seen this too," Naomi said softly. She caught Cheryl's eye. "I am sorry, Cheryl, if I have judged Anton too harshly, but as I said, you were not here when Liesel Hostettler disappeared. Her parents were heartbroken, as were Anton's mother and sister. We tried to support both families through that painful time." She put her hand on Rebecca's bright curls. "Perhaps you can understand a little more what it is like to lose a child now that you have one."

Cheryl's eyes immediately filled with unexpected tears. She couldn't imagine how she would feel if Rebecca went missing. She suddenly felt almost overwhelming compassion for Liesel's family.

"It was a terrible time," Levi acknowledged. "But it was awful for Anton as well. He was accused and convicted by many without any evidence."

"Did you say the girl's last name was Hostettler?" Sharon asked.

"Ja," Naomi said. "Liesel. The parents are Joel and Roseanna."

Sharon shook her head. "We have some Hostettlers in Bird-in-Hand. I wonder if they might be related. There are quite a few families in my town that once lived in Sugarcreek. I heard a lot about this place before coming here."

"Actually, we know quite a few families that moved here from Lancaster County," Seth said. "It has a large Amish community."

"Ja," Sharon said. "Migration is not unusual."

"I do not think Joel and Roseanna have much family," Levi said. "They never talked about anyone they were close to. Now they have isolated themselves. Even from the church. They seem to have given themselves over to their anger. They truly believe their daughter is lost to them forever and that Anton is responsible for her…demise."

"Perhaps it is best if we find another subject for conversation," Seth said firmly. "I apologize for discussing this in front of you," he said to Sharon. "We are usually more reserved in front of our guests."

Sharon shook her head. "Please do not alter your conversation for me. I may live with my mother, but I have seen many things over the years. Life does not always go the way we wish it to."

"Ja, this is true," Naomi said. "But sometimes life can also surprise you." She smiled at Rebecca. "Even when things don't work out the way you thought they would, *Gott* makes something beautiful. He has His own plans, and I am learning more and more to trust Him."

Although Cheryl's relationship with Levi had taken his parents by surprise, they couldn't be closer now. Cheryl really felt like Seth and Naomi's daughter.

"Maybe you could invite Anton to supper while he is here," Levi said.

Cheryl almost choked on a bite of roast. He was really pushing it.

Naomi hesitated. Cheryl was pretty sure there were people in Sugarcreek who wouldn't look kindly on the Millers allowing Anton Birken into their home. What would Naomi say? But even before she responded, Cheryl knew exactly how she would respond.

"I think we should do so," she said. She stuck her chin out and spoke with conviction even though Cheryl was certain it was difficult for her to extend an invitation to someone she didn't completely trust. Naomi was a good woman. The idea that Anton might have been unfairly accused was something she was considering now, and her sense of justice dictated that she do something about it.

Cheryl prayed that Naomi wouldn't regret her expression of grace.

CHAPTER SEVEN

Levi and Cheryl dropped Sharon off at the cottage before heading home. Sharon seemed okay but was rather quiet. Cheryl wondered if their conversation about Anton Birken had upset her. She thought about bringing it up, but she wasn't quite sure what to say. It was too bad Sharon's visit to Sugarcreek had coincided with Anton's return. Usually, Naomi was happy and easygoing. This evening, she'd been tense. Even though she was trying to have a good attitude about Anton, Cheryl could tell she was still concerned. Cheryl kept reminding herself that she had faith in Chief Twitchell and Pastor Lory. And Levi's decision to take Anton with him when he left the house helped. She actually felt quite a bit better about his visit.

Anton was supposed to arrive tomorrow afternoon. Cheryl planned to run to the grocery store in the morning since she assumed he'd eat most of his meals with them. She also wanted Sharon to join them for meals. Though the cottage was already stocked with basics, Cheryl had every intention of being a good hostess. She had written out a grocery list around some of her best dishes. Although she wasn't as good a cook as Naomi was, she'd gotten better with her mother-in-law's help. She had some pretty good recipes she thought Anton would like.

"Are you worried about Anton?" Levi asked as he turned their truck toward home.

"Not really," she said. "Thank you for making sure he isn't here when Rebecca and I are alone." She turned to look at her husband. "To be honest, I'm more concerned about the girl who disappeared. Has it occurred to anyone that if she met with some kind of violence, that person might still be in Sugarcreek?"

Levi nodded. "More than once. Anton was worried about it too."

"Was there anyone the police looked at?"

"Liesel was seen several times with an *Englischer*."

"Who was that?"

"Douglas Powell."

Cheryl's breath caught in her throat. She knew Douglas. He'd loaded her groceries more than once at the grocery store and had even delivered them when she was pregnant or when the weather was bad. He seemed like a nice person. Cheryl had never felt uncomfortable around him.

"Some people thought they planned to run away together. Douglas was the first person Chief Twitchell interviewed when Liesel disappeared, but he said he was not in town when she went missing. The chief could not prove otherwise."

"But he also couldn't prove he was telling the truth?"

Levi shook his head. "I believe Douglas said he was at a party. The host backed him up. Said he was there during the time Liesel went missing."

"Maybe that was a lie. Could he have...hurt her? Maybe Liesel never left Sugarcreek."

Levi sighed. "Believe me, the same thing occurred to me more than once, but the truth is, Douglas has been a good citizen. He has never done anything that made me suspicious. Anton told me that Liesel talked about running away more than once, but she did not tell him she was leaving that night."

"Do you believe they were romantically involved?"

"No. Anton always said they were just friends, and I believed him."

"But wouldn't she tell her friend she was going to run away?" Cheryl asked.

"You would think so." Levi tapped his fingers on the steering wheel. A sign he was bothered by something. "Liesel's parents said she was content at home. That there was no reason for her to leave. She had recently pledged herself to the church." He shrugged. "Anton said a few things that made me wonder how happy she really was, but he kept his conversations with Liesel to himself. I suspected she did not want her private feelings shared with anyone else."

"That really doesn't sound like someone who would run away, does it?"

Levi shook his head. "No, it does not. Of course, anything is possible, but it has been ten years. She would be an adult. Why has she not contacted her parents?"

"Why haven't you ever told me about Liesel?" Cheryl asked.

"Well, because there wasn't much to tell, and my actions at the time Anton was accused...embarrassed me. I did not want you to know your husband was a coward."

"Oh, Levi," Cheryl said, putting her hand on his arm. "That's not true. You're the bravest man I know."

He glanced at her and grinned. "I am glad you think so. It seems I have you fooled."

She slapped his arm and laughed.

"Liesel's parents left the church not long after she went missing. Many people tried to reach out to them, but they would not respond. I believe they are angry with God. Liesel was their only child."

"I don't understand. Why is it God's fault?"

Levi tossed her a smile. "I love that you do not understand their anger. Some people blame God when something bad happens. They believe their daughter is dead. That God did not protect her."

"That's sad," Cheryl said softly. "The devil is the one who kills, steals, and destroys. Not God."

"You know that, but the Hostettlers do not seem to."

Something occurred to Cheryl. "Oh, Levi. If they think Anton killed their daughter, what will they say when they find out he's in town? And staying with us?"

Levi shrugged. "I have thought about this, but what can we do? We cannot turn Anton away because of the Hostettlers, can we? Their anger is misplaced. Although I feel bad for them, I believe it is time for Anton to stop paying for something he had nothing to do with."

Cheryl was quiet for a moment. Finally, she said, "I'm sure you're right. But maybe we should visit with them before Anton shows up. Don't you think they should know?"

It was Levi's turn to be silent. "Ja, they should," he said finally, "but I do not relish the idea of confronting them."

"Should we ask the chief to inform them?"

"I want to say yes, but it may be my lack of bravery showing up again."

Cheryl chuckled softly. Rebecca had fallen asleep in her car seat, and Cheryl didn't want to wake her. "At least you're honest," she told Levi.

"*At least?*" he responded. "I hope you are also impressed by my many other sterling qualities."

"I really am." Cheryl grinned at her husband. "Why don't we visit the Hostettlers in the morning, before we go to the store? It shouldn't take long."

"I think that will work. I planned to help with the corn maze in the morning, but I am certain Eli can handle it."

"If Anton won't get here until after two o'clock, we should have plenty of time."

"I hope this will turn out the way Anton hopes," Levi said. "It seems he regrets not mending his relationship with his sister before his mother passed away."

"I pray it works out too," Cheryl said. "Surely after all these years his sister has softened her attitude toward him."

"I wish I could predict how she will act. I can still recall how angry she was. It was as if his being accused embarrassed her so much, she wanted nothing to do with him. I am not sure she ever believed he hurt that girl."

"That's really sad, isn't it?" Cheryl turned around to look at Rebecca's sweet face as she slept. "I hate the idea that anything like that could happen in our family."

"I feel the same way," Levi said. "We have weathered the storm of informing my parents of our engagement and of my decision to leave the Amish church. If we can come through that with our family intact, I believe we will be able to make it through anything."

"I agree," Cheryl said, reaching over and putting her hand on Levi's arm again. "I'm so blessed to be your wife and Rebecca's mother. We'll never let anything come between us."

Levi smiled at her. "I love you, my Cheryl."

"I love you too."

As they traveled the rest of the way home, Cheryl couldn't stop thinking about the two families broken by tragedy. Would Anton's visit make things worse? Or would it bring healing? She had no way of knowing the answer, but in her heart, Cheryl decided she'd do whatever she could to help these hurting people bind the wounds of the past.

CHAPTER EIGHT

Cheryl was up early the next morning, making breakfast and double-checking her list for the store. Yesterday afternoon, after Levi got back from fixing the roof on the dawdy haus, he'd watched Rebecca so Cheryl could make sure the house was clean. She had very little to do since she'd cleaned it so well after their last tenants. A little dusting and a quick run with the sweeper made it sparkle.

After Rebecca and Levi were through eating, she cleaned their daughter up and got her dressed to go out. Levi took care of a few chores and met them at the truck a little before ten o'clock. He had checked on the fields to make sure their fall crop was doing well. They grew alfalfa, corn, and soybeans. They also owned horses, cows, and a few sheep. Feeding them every day took some time.

Since they couldn't call the Hostettlers, they had no choice but to just show up. It was about ten fifteen when they pulled up to their house. It was a simple white farmhouse, not unlike other Amish homes in the area. Horses watched them from their corral. The family's buggy was parked on one side of the house. Cheryl was a little surprised, since they'd left the Amish church. It appeared they'd kept their Amish ways.

Levi took Rebecca from her car seat while Cheryl climbed out of the truck. She had butterflies in her stomach. Telling this family that Anton Birken was coming to town today felt like a heavy burden. She could only hope they'd made peace with what had happened. At that moment, she wished they'd asked Chief Twitchell to talk to the Hostettlers. It might have been the wiser choice.

They walked up onto the porch, and Levi knocked on the door. A few seconds later, it swung open. A large man stood there, his beard and clothing making him appear Amish. Maybe he hadn't left the church after all.

"Mr. Hostettler," Levi said, "I am Levi Miller and this is my wife, Cheryl, and our daughter, Rebecca. I wonder if we might have a few minutes of your time? We have something we need to tell you."

The man frowned at him for a few seconds before pulling the door all the way open. "Please come in," he said.

As they entered the house, a woman came around the corner. She wore a prayer kapp and her dress was simple, dark blue with a white apron.

"I am Joel and this is my wife, Roseanna. What can we do for you?"

"Joel," his wife said, "let them sit down. My goodness, where are your manners?" She smiled at Cheryl. "I recognize you. I have shopped in your store many times. We love all the wonderful items you sell. Especially the baked goods."

Cheryl recognized her too. Outside of casual pleasantries, they'd never really talked. Roseanna gestured toward the couch, so they sat down.

"It's good to see you again," Cheryl said. "I hope we're not disturbing you."

"Not at all," Roseanna said. "Can I get you some coffee?"

"Not for me," Levi said.

Cheryl shook her head. "No, thank you."

Joel sat down across from them. "What can we do for you?"

Levi cleared his throat. "We felt it was right to tell you something. You know that Ada Birken just passed away?"

"Yes," Joel said. "We have heard. We do not attend the church anymore, but we still have friends who are active. They told us of Ada's passing."

"You have not left the faith?" Levi asked.

"No," he replied. "We simply will not attend a church where people who are supposed to be our brothers and sisters have turned their backs on us."

Levi frowned. "I do not understand."

The couple looked at each other. Then Joel said, "You remember when our daughter, Liesel, went missing?"

Levi nodded.

"Anton Birken was an unwelcome presence in her life. We forbade him to see her, but he continued to meet with her secretly. We did not know this until it was too late."

"So you blame him for your daughter's disappearance?" Cheryl asked.

"Ja, we do. We could not get the chief of police to believe us. Even our bishop did not support us."

"Why do you think that is?" Levi asked.

"They told us there was no evidence Anton was anywhere near her the day she went missing. But we know better. We are certain Liesel met with him on the last day we saw her."

"How do you know that?" Cheryl asked.

"Every time she snuck out of the house without telling us where she was going she went to see him. They used to meet at the old Noffsinger house. The day she disappeared, she slipped out her bedroom window. She left behind a note Anton wrote, asking her to meet him there."

"But no one could prove he actually wrote that note, right?" Cheryl said. "Isn't that rather shaky evidence? I understand it was typewritten. On a computer. Anton didn't own a computer."

"That was the same thing the police said back then," Joel said. "But they were just covering for the boy. The note was obviously from him."

The Noffsinger house was not far from Levi and Cheryl's farm. It was an abandoned farmhouse once owned by an Amish widow who died without relatives. Although it was now owned by the widow's church, no one had done anything with it. It was in bad shape, probably not worth repairing. The church had decided recently to tear it down but planned to take care of it in the spring, when the weather improved. Although Cheryl hated to see the once-lovely old house destroyed, it was such an eyesore, she would be relieved to see it gone.

"I think Chief Twitchell would need more proof than that before he could accuse Anton," Cheryl said gently. "It's only fair."

Joel scowled at her. "We do not need an Englischer's law to tell us what is right. Anton Birken was responsible for our daughter's disappearance. Someday we will see him again, and we will get the truth from him."

Cheryl gulped nervously. Although the Amish didn't believe in violence, this sounded like a threat. Rebecca, who had been wiggling like a worm on her daddy's lap, jumped down and ran to Joel, holding her arms out. The fierce-looking Amish man's face crumbled, and he reached out for Rebecca, who jumped up into his arms. Although Levi and Cheryl had told Rebecca more than once not to run to strangers, she seemed to know when someone needed affection. She wrapped her arms around Joel's neck as tears dripped down his face. Obviously, he was thinking of his own daughter. Cheryl's heart broke for him and his wife as she wondered how she would feel if she were in his shoes.

"I am afraid we have drifted into something you do not need to worry about," Joel said, obviously trying to rein in his emotions. He put Rebecca down on the floor. "What did you come here to tell us?"

Levi looked at Cheryl. It was obvious he was struggling. Rebecca ran to Cheryl, and she gathered her daughter up into her arms.

"This is difficult for me to say," Levi said slowly, "but it is right that you should know. Anton is coming to Sugarcreek for his mother's funeral."

Roseanna cried out and put her hand over her mouth. Joel's face turned dark.

"We do not want him here," he said.

"I understand," Levi replied, "but surely you can understand that he desires to say goodbye to his mother."

"We do not," Joel said. "His sister will not want him here. She wants nothing to do with him."

"Do you believe she thinks Anton had something to do with your daughter's disappearance?" Cheryl asked.

Roseanna shook her head. "I honestly do not know. Anton was a troublemaker even before Liesel disappeared. He brought his mother much unhappiness. After he left, she changed. Became quiet. Did not smile much. Meredith says it is because Anton broke her heart. Their mother died not ever seeing him again. That may be why Meredith does not want to see him now. She may feel his visit is too late."

"Regardless, I am afraid he will be here," Levi said firmly. "I do not know if his sister will want him at the funeral. That is between them. Our concern was that you might be surprised to see him. We felt it was right to warn you."

Joel stood up and strode over to the window. He gazed outside for a few moments, not saying anything. Then he turned back to look at them. "I assume he is staying in a local motel? Surely, no one here would give him sanctuary. Knowing how we would feel about it."

"People forget, Joel," his wife said soothingly. "We have not been to church for a long time. They may not take our pain into consideration."

Levi cleared his throat. "The truth is, Anton will be staying in our dawdy haus. It is vacant at the moment. Chief Twitchell and our pastor asked us to give Anton a place to stay while he is here. Perhaps we should not have said yes, but I hoped after all these years, giving him temporary shelter would not cause strife. I hope you understand why we agreed to this. We have no desire to cause you further pain."

Joel turned his back to Levi. "Please leave my home," he said in a low voice. "And do not return."

"Brother, I do not want there to be animosity between us." Levi stood up and started toward him.

Joel swung his head around. There was anger in his expression and fury in his eyes. Levi took a step back.

"We are not *brothers*," Joel spat out. "Get out of my house. Now."

Rebecca, who had been watching the scene unfold before her, started to cry. Cheryl stood up and carried her to the door, joining Levi there.

"We will pray for you," Levi said, his hand on the doorknob.

The Hostettlers didn't answer. Cheryl, Levi, and Rebecca stepped out on the front porch. Levi was trembling. Confrontation was difficult for him. For anyone raised Amish.

"Everything will be okay, Levi," Cheryl said. "Joel's anger is his own. We don't need to let it affect us."

Levi sighed. "I do not like being in the middle of this. This couple is grieving. If something happened to Rebecca..."

"Dada, Dada, Dada..." Rebecca recited over and over. She reached for him and Levi took her, holding her close.

He didn't say anything else. There was nothing else that needed to be said.

Chapter Nine

Levi and Cheryl didn't talk much on the way to the store. The grief Cheryl had seen in the Hostettlers' faces fought against her belief that Anton deserved to be seen as innocent until he was proven guilty.

"Levi, are we sure we're doing the right thing?" she asked finally.

He hesitated a moment before saying, "Yes, I believe so, Cheryl. I knew Anton. Yes, he could be a little wild, but only because he was not certain the Amish life was for him. Everyone must make his or her own decision. It cannot be based on your parents' beliefs or on what is comfortable for you. His mother wanted him to be a good Amish boy. His questions confused her." He shrugged. "We used to talk. I had many of the same questions he did, although I did not leave the church."

"Until I dragged you away," Cheryl said under her breath.

"You did not drag me away. I made my own decision. And Anton made his."

Cheryl frowned. "But I thought Anton left because people in the church accused him of hurting Liesel?"

Levi shook his head. "He had already decided to leave, but he told me he was going to wait a while. Until he could get his mother to understand. He had no desire to hurt her. He loved her."

"So he left after Liesel disappeared?"

"Ja. He told me he believed it would easier for his mother if he was gone."

"But it wasn't."

Levi shook his head. "No, it was not. I would rather have Rebecca with us so we could deal with any problems rather than have her just take off. Unfortunately, Anton made a different choice. But he really was trying to protect his mother."

"That's so sad." Cheryl sighed. She looked back at Rebecca, who was snuggling her baby doll. Cheryl couldn't help but think about the misunderstandings she'd had with her parents down through the years. The times of conflict when she'd actually looked forward to moving far enough away from them so she wouldn't have to see them as much. Would Rebecca feel this way about her and Levi someday? The prospect distressed her.

"Do you feel prepared for Anton's visit?" Levi asked.

"Yes, I cleaned the dawdy haus yesterday. After we go to the store, I'll stock the kitchen. Then everything will be ready."

Levi frowned at her. "I thought the dawdy haus was already clean. I remember you cleaning it after our last visitors."

Cheryl sighed. "Yes, I did. But I wanted it to be...visitor clean."

Levi arched one eyebrow. "And does our home live up to *visitor* clean? What do we have? *Family* clean? A step below what you do for strangers?"

"Very funny. We have...*relaxed* clean. We have *toddler* clean."

Levi snorted. "No matter how you say it, I feel as if we are being treated as second-class citizens."

"Very funny. I take pretty good care of us, and I'm getting better and better as a cook."

Levi sighed dramatically. "A ringing endorsement of your talents. *Pretty good* and *getting better.*"

Cheryl giggled. "You need to be careful. I might take you seriously one of these days and get mad."

Levi laughed. "I will not rate you as a wife, but I will tell you that there is no house in the world I would rather live in than one that has you and Rebecca in it."

"I know that," Cheryl said gently.

Levi's gentle teasing had helped to get her mind off of Anton and the Hostettlers for a moment. Probably his intent.

Levi pulled up in front of the large grocery store on the edge of town. They liked shopping at the Swiss Village Market, in Sugarcreek, but it didn't carry everything the large store did. The three of them got out and went inside. Levi guided the grocery cart with Rebecca sitting in the space at the front of the cart designed for children. To Rebecca, a trip to the grocery store was an adventure. She laughed and pointed at everything she saw that tickled her fancy. Cheryl turned around when she heard someone call her name. Douglas Powell stood behind them, putting some items into the meat display case.

"How are you?" he asked with a smile.

Cheryl immediately felt guilty. They'd been talking about him as if he were a criminal, but the truth was, he was always nice to Cheryl and usually paid attention to Rebecca.

"We are doing fine, Douglas. How are you?" Levi said, covering for Cheryl's momentary silence.

Douglas put the rest of the packages of meat he'd been holding in the case and straightened up. Then he walked over to where they stood. He grinned at Rebecca, and she laughed at him.

"She's getting bigger and bigger," he said. "How old is she now?"

"Seventeen months," Cheryl said. Her stomach was in knots, and she wanted to get Rebecca as far away from Douglas as she could. Yet she knew there wasn't any real reason for it.

He wiggled his finger at Rebecca and then lightly poked her in the tummy, making her laugh. "She's really cute." He turned his attention from Rebecca and smiled at them. "Anything I can help you find?"

"No," Cheryl said quickly. "I think we're good. It's good to see you, Douglas." She turned around and began to push the cart down the aisle. She heard Levi say something to Douglas and then he caught up with her.

"You were a little rude to him," he said softly.

"I'm sorry. He makes me nervous."

"Because of what was said at supper? Remember, he wasn't in town when Liesel disappeared. I believe you are seeing him in an unfair light."

Cheryl turned the corner and found the chocolate syrup. She took a bottle down from the shelf and put it in her cart. "He *says* he wasn't in town." She sighed. "I'm sorry to sound so suspicious. You're probably right. All this talk about a missing girl. As the mother of a girl, it seems to be getting to me, Levi."

He leaned over and kissed the top of her head. "I understand, but Rebecca is not Liesel Hostettler. She is safe and sound. And she will stay so."

"I'm sure the Hostettlers thought the same thing."

Levi didn't respond as Cheryl pushed the cart down the aisle and turned in to the next one. She grabbed two cartons of oatmeal, one for Sharon and one for them since they were getting low.

"Perhaps I have made an error in judgment," Levi said suddenly. "If this causes you too much distress we should rescind our offer to let Anton stay with us."

Cheryl stopped and looked at him. She suddenly felt bad about making him second-guess his decision. "No, you're doing the right thing. I'm sorry. I've allowed all this talk to get to me. You're right. What happened to Liesel has nothing to do with us. Forgive me for being too sensitive. Anton is welcome to stay with us."

"You are not too sensitive. You are a wonderful mother who loves her child. Liesel's story is very upsetting. I should have realized it would bother you."

"Well, like Sharon said, life doesn't always go the way we want it to."

"This is true," Levi said. "I forget because my life is going just the way I want."

Cheryl smiled at him. "You're right. We're very blessed."

"Ja, we are."

Cheryl continued through her list, getting everything she needed. Sharon was coming to supper tonight. She wanted to invite Anton as well. Of course, he could be tired from driving all day and might want to rest his first night in town.

She picked out some deli meats and cheeses for sandwiches he could make for himself if he wanted to. She also selected chips, fruit, coffee, muffins, bread, and peanut butter.

"Anything else he might like?" she asked Levi.

"Hard for me to say," he answered. "I haven't seen him in a long time." His forehead wrinkled in thought. "He used to like chocolate chip cookies. How about baking him some?"

"Wait a minute," Cheryl said. "Chocolate chip cookies are *your* favorite. Are you thinking of Anton or yourself?"

Levi gave her a look of over-exaggerated innocence. "I have no idea what you are talking about."

Cheryl laughed. "Follow me." She hurried over to the aisle with cookies and picked up a package. "I'll bake some later," she said. "My cookies are better than these, but at least he'll have some until I have time to bake a batch."

"I sometimes ask you for cookies, and you tell me you are too busy," he said, scowling. "I am beginning to realize that I am at the bottom of your list."

She reached up and kissed him on the cheek, something that still embarrassed him a little in public. A reaction from his past. However, now he tolerated her attention. "You really are pitiful. How about I double the chocolate chip recipe and make plenty for you? Will that ease your pain?"

His frown turned into a goofy smile. "I think it just might take care of it."

Cheryl grinned at him. Somehow, Rebecca picked up that her daed was being funny, and she giggled, which made Cheryl and Levi laugh.

They finished up their shopping, checked out, and pushed the cart out to the car. Cheryl kept looking for Douglas, hoping he wasn't going to come to help them. Thankfully, he didn't turn up.

As they drove out of the parking lot, she saw him assisting another customer with her cart. He stopped and stared at their truck as they pulled out onto the road.

CHAPTER TEN

Cheryl and Sharon got to the Swiss Miss around noon. Instantly, Cheryl could tell by Esther's expression that something was wrong. She took her coat off and hung it up. After taking off Rebecca's coat, she went over to the counter where Esther stood.

"What's going on?" she asked Esther in a low voice.

"One of Sharon's quilts has gone missing," she whispered. "I had them out, was putting them up on our quilt hangers. I went to the office for just a minute. When I came back, one of them was gone."

"Which one?" Cheryl asked, alarmed by the news.

"The child's quilt."

Cheryl was surprised to hear that a quilt could be stolen without someone seeing it happen. Even though the child's quilt was smaller than the other two, it was still large enough to cover a twin bed.

"Who was in the store when you went into the office?" Cheryl whispered. She glanced over at Sharon. She was looking around the store, far enough away not to hear them.

"Several people. Kathy from the Honey Bee. Gail Murray..." Esther frowned as she tried to remember. "There were a couple of strangers. A man and his wife. There wasn't anything about them that made me suspicious."

"Call Kathy and Gail. Ask them if they saw anything suspicious." She glanced around the room. "Are you absolutely certain you didn't misplace it? Put it somewhere else?"

Esther shook her head. Her eyes were shiny with tears. "I've searched everywhere. Besides, why would I move it? I was putting it up for display."

Cheryl sighed. "Let's not say anything to Sharon yet. First of all, make those calls. Hopefully, one of them saw something. If we can't find it, we'll have to call the police."

"I am so sorry, Cheryl. I should not have left the store unattended."

Cheryl hugged the distraught girl. "We've both done it many times, Esther. We don't expect our customers to be thieves. Don't blame yourself. Let's just find the quilt."

Esther wiped away a tear that fell down her cheek. "You are very kind, but I am responsible. If the quilt is not recovered, I will cover the cost."

That was easy to say, but handmade Amish quilts went for very high prices. If Cheryl allowed her to take responsibility for it, which she wouldn't, Esther would be working off that quilt for a long time. "You're not responsible, Esther. The person who took it is. I have no intention of letting you pay for it if we don't find it. But thank you."

She started to walk away but realized that if she and Sharon were going to lunch at the Honey Bee, she could talk to Kathy

Kimble herself. She turned back and told Esther to call Gail, the owner of Buttons 'n Bows, a cute shop down the street that specialized in purses and accessories. "I'll check back with you after I talk to Kathy. And if you find the quilt in the meantime, call me right away, okay? You and Joni go through the entire store. Every nook and cranny."

Esther nodded. The door to the store opened, and Joni came in to start her shift. She headed their way.

"Tell Joni not to say anything to anyone else," Cheryl told Esther. "I'd like to keep this between us…at least for a while."

"All right," Esther said.

Cheryl greeted Joni, who stared at Esther. It was obvious Esther was upset.

Just then, the bell over the door rang again and Naomi came in. She greeted them with a wide smile that faded when she saw their faces. Sharon was coming their way, so Cheryl shook her head just slightly so Naomi wouldn't say anything to alert Sharon that something was wrong. Cheryl felt a little guilty not telling Sharon right away that one of her quilts was missing, but she couldn't shake the hope that it had accidentally been misplaced. Esther seemed so sure she hadn't moved it somewhere else, but Cheryl had thought the same thing many times and found the missing item later. All she could do was pray this would work out the same way.

"We're going to the Honey Bee for lunch," she told Naomi. "Do you have time to join us?"

"I would love to come," Naomi said. "As long as I am not in the way."

Cheryl smiled and gave her mother-in-law a hug. "You are never, ever in the way."

"I am looking forward to seeing the Honey Bee," Sharon said. "You have told me such wonderful things about it."

"You'll love it," Cheryl said. "Let's go."

Sharon headed to the front door with Naomi and Cheryl behind her. Cheryl grabbed Naomi and pulled her close, whispering in her ear, "We've lost one of Sharon's quilts."

Naomi's eyes got big. "You have not told Sharon?"

"No, I'm hoping we can find it before I have to. I think Kathy and Gail were in the store when it went missing. I want to talk to them first. Before I call Chief Twitchell."

"Do you think that is wise?" Naomi whispered.

Cheryl could hear the doubt in her voice. Was she doing the right thing? Was she giving the thief time to get away? She wished Levi were here. He'd know what to do.

"If Kathy or Gail don't know anything about it, I'll call him."

"Gail Murray?"

"Yes," Cheryl said. She and Naomi reached Sharon, who was waiting on the front porch. "What do you recommend?" Sharon asked.

"Recommend?" Cheryl asked. She realized right away what Sharon was asking and laughed at herself. "Sorry. I was distracted. You mean at the Honey Bee." She smiled at Sharon. "Everything is good. Why don't you look over the menu and let me know what sounds interesting. If you have a hard time choosing, I'll let you know which item I'd pick."

"That sounds good," Sharon said. She looked back and forth between Cheryl and Naomi. "Is everything all right? You seem rather preoccupied."

"There's a problem at the store," Cheryl said. "Let's get some lunch. Maybe by the time we've finished, the situation will have sorted itself out."

Sharon nodded. "I hope it will. You have such a wonderful shop. I am happy to think my quilts will be part of your inventory."

Naomi's expression made it clear she wasn't comfortable with Cheryl not telling Sharon what had happened, but Cheryl still couldn't believe someone could actually walk out of the store with a quilt and no one notice.

They walked across the street to the Honey Bee Café. The restaurant was housed in a charming building, painted dark gray with white accents. It had a large front porch with tables available for those heartier souls who felt like braving the chilly temperatures. When they got inside, the aromas from the kitchen made Cheryl instantly hungry. A few minutes ago, she felt as if she couldn't possibly eat. She was too worried. But now her stomach growled with anticipation.

Business was bustling. The inside of the restaurant was just as appealing as the outside. Homey decorations and café-styled chairs and tables dotted the main room where the counter was located. A large menu was posted behind the counter. The attached room had booths and continued with the warm ambiance Kathy had worked hard to create. Sharon was looking over the menu, but she seemed uncertain.

"Everything is good, Sharon," Cheryl assured her. "My favorites are the bacon-apple-cheddar grilled sandwich and the Mediterranean wrap. They also have the most awesome homemade applesauce. And for dessert, you've got to try the coffee cake or the honey walnut baklava."

"I like tomato soup," Sharon said. "Is their tomato basil bisque soup good?"

"The best I have ever had," Naomi said. "Even I cannot make it as good as this."

Sharon smiled. "That sounds like quite a recommendation. I believe I will try the soup. And perhaps the baklava for dessert."

"Great choices," Cheryl said.

She ordered the bacon-apple-cheddar sandwich, and Naomi asked for the patty melt with a small bowl of tomato soup.

Cheryl smiled at Andrea, the assistant manager who was taking their order. "If they're both getting the tomato soup, I can't be left out. I'll take a bowl too."

Andrea laughed. "It's certainly popular. We sell a lot of it."

"It's delicious."

"Thanks. Have a seat. We'll bring it to your table when it's ready."

The women thanked her and went to look for a table. Although the café was crowded, they managed to find a booth in the adjoining room. Once they were settled, Cheryl excused herself. She went back to the counter and asked Andrea if Kathy was there. Before Andrea could answer, Kathy came around the corner from the back. She smiled when she saw Cheryl.

"Glad to see you, Cheryl. I was just in your store earlier."

"I know. Could I talk to you a moment? Alone?"

"Of course." Kathy walked over to a small table near the front window where no one was sitting. She motioned for Cheryl to sit down.

"Now what can I do for you?" Kathy asked.

Cheryl told her about the missing quilt. "I haven't called the police yet because I keep hoping there's a simple explanation. But I have to do something soon if I can't locate it."

Kathy's eyes widened, and she leaned in close to Cheryl. "You need to call the police right away. There have been several thefts on Main Street in the past few days. Someone broke in through our back door two nights ago and took some food. Some of the shops have had clothing items go missing."

"Food? I can see why they'd take a valuable quilt. It could be sold. But food and clothing? It just doesn't make sense." She sighed. "I'll call Chief Twitchell and tell him what's happened. I really hoped it was a mistake. If we can't find the quilt I'll have to reimburse the woman who made it."

"Maybe a description of the thief will help," Kathy said.

Cheryl's mouth dropped open in surprise. "You...you saw who took the quilt?"

"Yes," Kathy said. "And I'd be happy to describe her to the police."

CHAPTER ELEVEN

Cheryl was shocked. "You actually saw someone steal the quilt?" She knew she was repeating herself, but she had a hard time understanding why Kathy hadn't said anything at the time. Maybe they could have caught the thief and recovered the quilt.

Kathy nodded. "I had no idea she was stealing it though. I assumed she'd bought it. I have to admit I thought it was a little odd it wasn't in a bag or a box, but it was rather large, so I figured it was too big to fit into any kind of wrapping you had available."

"What did she look like?" Cheryl asked.

"She was a young woman. Maybe twenty, twenty-five. At first, I thought she was with her husband or boyfriend. But now I'm not so sure."

"Can I ask why?"

"She followed him around the store. And when he left, she walked out behind him. But at the time I thought it was odd that he didn't seem to interact with her. I ended up wondering if they were really together." She reached over and put her hand on Cheryl's arm. "I'm not saying they weren't. I'm just not sure." She sighed. "If I'd had any idea she was stealing from you, I would have said something right away." She took her hand away and shook her head. "To be honest, the woman didn't look like a thief. She looked like..." Kathy paused a moment. Then she said, "She looked like someone's daughter. I know that sounds weird but..."

"No, I understand. She looked like someone who was raised by good parents. Someone who wouldn't steal."

"Yes," Kathy said. "I'm so sorry, Cheryl. I feel awful. I could have stopped her."

"You can't be expected to know if someone is a thief by looking at them, Kathy. It wouldn't have occurred to me either. Please don't worry about it." Cheryl paused for a moment, trying to figure out what to do next. "Would you be able to describe her to Chief Twitchell?"

"Yes, I'm sure I could."

Cheryl rubbed her hands together. "I'm going to call the police station. And I'm going to have to fess up to Sharon."

At her look of confusion, Cheryl said, "Sharon Vogel is here from Bird-in-Hand, Pennsylvania. She made the quilt."

"I really hope the police catch that woman, Cheryl. I'll be praying that the quilt is found."

Cheryl managed to give Kathy a forced smile. "Thank you. I could use all the prayer I can get."

"Tell the chief I'll be glad to give a description of the girl I saw."

"Thanks. I'd better get back to Sharon and Naomi. I guess I need to make a call first though."

Kathy stood up. "I'd better get back to work anyway. Please, keep me updated on what happens. I'm wondering if this girl is responsible for the other thefts around here. Including my break-in."

"She might be," Cheryl said. "I guess we'll have to let Chief Twitchell sort it out." Rather than go right back to the table, Cheryl stepped outside onto the porch and called the police station. The phone was answered by Delores Delgado, the department's receptionist.

"Hi, Delores. Is the chief available?"

"Sorry, Cheryl. He's out investigating a theft. We've had several complaints lately about things missing from our local stores."

"Actually, that's why I called. I guess you can add the Swiss Miss to the list. We're missing a quilt."

"A quilt? How does someone sneak out of your store carrying a quilt? Did they break in over night?"

"No. I guess our customers are too trusting. They thought the woman who took it had paid for it."

"Please tell me someone saw her and can give us a description."

"Yeah, someone did," Cheryl said. "Kathy Kimble was in the store and got a good look at her. I thought the chief might like to talk to Kathy."

Delores snorted. "He'll be thrilled. This is the first time anyone has gotten a good look at the thief. Where are you now?"

"I'm at the Honey Bee."

"I take it you didn't see this woman?" Delores asked.

"No, I wasn't there. Esther Miller saw her, but she was busy with another customer and only glanced at her. Esther thought she might be with a man and assumed it was her husband, but I'm not sure about that."

"Her husband?" Delores paused for a moment. "Maybe it's a team. I hope Kathy can describe him as well."

"I don't know, but I assume she can."

"Okay. I'll contact the chief and send him to talk to Kathy. We'll need you to fill out an incident report."

"Okay. No problem. I'll get by there sometime today."

Cheryl said goodbye to Delores and disconnected the call. She took a steadying breath and went back inside the café. She had to tell Sharon what had happened before she found out when the chief showed up. She went back to the table where Naomi and Sharon waited for her. She slid into the booth next to Naomi.

"Is everything all right?" Sharon asked.

Before she could answer, Annie, one of Kathy's waitresses, showed up with their lunch. Cheryl waited until everyone had been served. She'd been looking forward to her meal, but now she'd lost her appetite.

"Sharon," she said finally, "there's something I have to tell you." She nervously cleared her throat. "I don't want you to think I'm irresponsible or that my staff is incompetent. But... Well, somehow someone took one of your quilts out of my store. We have a description of the person, and I've notified the police. I probably should have called sooner, but I kept hoping we'd just misplaced it. Unfortunately, it seems we have a small crime spree happening downtown." She swallowed hard and met Sharon's eyes. "I'm so sorry. Of course I'll reimburse you for the full amount the quilt is worth." She tried to blink away the tears that suddenly sprang into her eyes. "It's such a beautiful quilt, I'm sorry one of our customers won't have the chance to enjoy it." She stopped to take a ragged breath. "I want you to know this kind of thing isn't usual for us. I—"

Sharon reached over and put her hand on Cheryl's. "Please, I understand. Maybe the poor soul who took the quilt needed it more than we did. We need to pray it will bring them comfort."

Cheryl, who had spent a lot of time with the Amish, was still surprised from time to time by their gentle spirits and generous attitudes. She shook her head. "Thank you, Sharon. I still insist you allow me to pay you for the quilt, but your reaction brings me great comfort. I was so concerned you would lose faith in me."

"Oh, Cheryl," Sharon said with a smile, "I see a wonderful person who cares deeply about the people in her life. I am honored to have my quilts in your store. This incident is not your fault and does not change my view of you in the slightest. I choose to believe the person who took my quilt needed it. Let it be my gift to them. You do not owe me anything."

"Thank you, but I'm afraid in this situation, I must insist. You can give the money away if you wish."

"If it is important to you," Sharon said, "I will abide by your wishes."

"It's very important to me."

Sharon went back to eating her lunch. "This is very good," she said. "I am so glad we came here. I do not get out much at home."

Naomi laughed lightly. "It was the same with me until Cheryl came to Sugarcreek. Most of the time I cooked at home. I am grateful that my world is a little larger now because of her."

Cheryl was touched by Naomi's comment. "And here I'm thinking you're the one who's expanded my life."

Sharon smiled at them. "I am encouraged by your love for each other. I have seen families torn apart because of love outside of the faith." She shrugged. "Love is nothing without forgiveness and understanding. Unfortunately, not everyone who lives an Amish life walks that kind of love."

Naomi nodded. "We have had our challenges, but Cheryl and I were friends before she married Levi." She patted Cheryl's shoulder. "That friendship carried us through. Now I am blessed to find my best friend is family. What could be better?"

"Kathy's baklava?" Cheryl said, her appetite restored.

The women laughed.

Cheryl was getting ready to take a bite of her sandwich when she noticed Chief Twitchell walk into the dining room. She wasn't sure if he was looking for her, but she waved anyway. For a few minutes, she'd forgotten about the missing quilt. But as the chief headed her way, the reality of the missing quilt returned. The Honey Bee's great food felt like lead in her stomach.

Chapter Twelve

The chief slid into the booth next to Sharon. Cheryl introduced them.

"Happy to meet you, ma'am," he said. He turned his attention to Cheryl. "Are you missin' anything except a quilt?"

"Not that I know of," Cheryl said. "I'll ask Esther to take an inventory."

"That might be wise. Lots of reports of things taken from shops downtown." He shook his head. "Nothin' too expensive. Food. Clothes. Now a blanket."

"It was an Amish handmade *quilt*," Cheryl said. "Not a blanket. It might be worth a little less because of its size, but I would probably have put a value of eight to nine hundred dollars on it."

The chief's eyebrows arched. "Sorry. I misunderstood. Didn't realize it was a handmade quilt. I know they're expensive. My wife saw one she wanted, but it was sixteen hundred dollars. Too much for a police chief's salary."

Cheryl nodded. "You can see why I'm so upset." She indicated Sharon sitting next to him. "This is Sharon Vogel. She made the quilt."

"I'm sorry, ma'am," he said to her.

"I told Cheryl not to worry about it," Sharon said. "But she feels responsible, even though I do not see it that way."

"That's very gracious of you," the chief said. "But unfortunately, this isn't the only missin' item." He pulled a small notebook out of his pocket and flipped the pages until he seemed to find what he was looking for. "With this quilt, the tally is over twenty-five hundred dollars' worth of stuff that's disappeared from various stores. That's a lot."

"The kinds of things stolen seems odd," Naomi said.

"I was thinking the same thing," Cheryl said. "Clothes, food, a quilt. Almost as if the thief took things she needed to take care of herself."

"I guess she could sell the quilt for a nice amount of money," the chief said.

"Yeah," Cheryl agreed, "but it's been chilly lately. What if she took it to stay warm?"

"Maybe," the chief said slowly. "I want to get a description of the quilt out right away though. In case someone tries to sell it." He looked at Sharon. "Can you describe it, ma'am?"

While Sharon gave the chief details about the quilt, Cheryl thought about the thefts. To her, it sounded like someone who was hungry and needed clothing and warmth. So what was next? She wasn't sure, but the Swiss Miss carried a lot of baked goods and candy. Was it possible that would be the thief's next target? When they got back to the shop, she'd tell Esther and Joni to keep a close eye on their food items. She wanted to find the young woman and get the quilt back. She could deal with missing food, but Sharon's beautiful quilt was something else. No matter how forgiving Sharon was, it represented hours of work and dedication. It was precious, and it was stolen from Cheryl's store. That made it her problem.

The chief finished writing down Sharon's description and put his notebook away. "I'd better get goin'," he said. "If I find out anything, I'll contact you." He got out of the booth and stood next to it. "Anton arrives today, right?"

"Yes," Cheryl said. "Levi's at home, waiting for him."

The chief tipped his hat at them and said to Sharon, "It was nice meetin' you, ma'am. I'll do my best to find your quilt."

Sharon thanked him, and he went into the other room, probably looking for Kathy.

A little while later, Kathy came up to the table. "I talked to the chief. Hopefully, my description will help them find this woman. Replacing my back door wasn't cheap."

"Don't you find it odd?" Cheryl said. "I mean, the things that are being taken?"

"I do," said Kathy. "We actually had some money in the back. A deposit that hadn't been made yet. It wasn't touched. Just food. I thought it was strange too."

Cheryl picked up her fork. "If I hear anything from the chief, I'll let you know."

"I'll do the same. Thanks, Cheryl."

As Kathy walked back toward the kitchen, Naomi sighed. "I am beginning to feel a little sorry for our thief."

Cheryl should have been surprised, but she wasn't. That was Naomi. She was compassionate above all, a quality Cheryl wished she had more of.

Sharon spoke up. "I feel the same way. It is as if she is just trying to survive."

Cheryl shook her head and looked back and forth between them. "A lot of people have problems, but they don't steal to take care of themselves."

"But for the grace of Gott..." Naomi said.

Cheryl couldn't hide a smile. Even though she couldn't completely agree with Naomi's kindhearted response to the situation, she appreciated her. She sometimes felt her mother-in-law's benevolence was responsible for the lion's share of their relationship. Cheryl had asked God more than once to make her more like Naomi. She hoped He was answering that prayer, but she wasn't sure she'd ever be the kind of woman Naomi was.

The women finished their meal and went back to the Swiss Miss. Esther had finished putting up the other quilt Sharon had brought with her. It was mounted on the wall behind the counter. Cheryl had put a price of fourteen hundred dollars on it. Even at that amount, she was confident it would sell quickly.

Naomi told them she had to get home. She had orders for cheese and jelly that needed to be filled. Cheryl hugged her, and Naomi left. She and Sharon went into Cheryl's office. They settled on a business plan.

"I wish you could make these quilts faster," Cheryl said with a smile. "But I realize they wouldn't have the same quality. You just send me what you can."

"I can give you at least four quilts a year," Sharon said. "I can make more, but I also sell them in Bird-in-Hand. I have to keep my other commitments."

"I totally understand," Cheryl said. "Esther called your friend in Bird-in-Hand. She promised to talk to your mother about the other three quilts. I'm hoping they'll get here before the festival. As far as what else you can send me when you get home, I feel blessed to get anything from you. Especially after losing that other quilt." Cheryl reached into her desk drawer and took out a checkbook. "I'd like to give you nine hundred for the quilt. Does that sound fair to you? If you want more, just tell me."

Sharon shook her head. "Can we at least split the loss?"

Cheryl shook her head. "I can't. I'm sorry. I'm also writing you a check for the quilt that sold. Please allow me to pay you for the missing quilt. If you don't want to keep the money, that's up to you. But I feel very strongly about taking responsibility for what happened."

Sharon sighed and took the check Cheryl held out. "I will do as you ask. I must say, you are very stubborn."

Cheryl grinned. "I've heard that more than once. From my husband, my mother and father, my brother... The list goes on."

Sharon grinned. "I suspect they are right."

"And I suspect *you're* right."

They laughed.

Cheryl was glad to see Sharon put the check into her pocket. The money wouldn't make up for the loss of the beautiful quilt, but at least it helped to relieve some of Cheryl's feelings of guilt. She was grateful Sharon was still willing to work with her.

"Would you like to visit some of the shops around town?" Cheryl asked. "I'd be happy to show you some of Sugarcreek."

"When do you need to go home?" Sharon asked.

"I'm sure Levi is having fun with Rebecca. He won't mind if we take some time to poke around. I do need to stop by the police station and fill out that incident report, but it should only take a few minutes."

"What time is your guest supposed to arrive?"

"Sometime after two. I'm not sure, but I assume once he gets to the house, he'll need time to unpack and rest. We'll meet him tonight at supper."

"Well, I must admit I would like to see the large cuckoo clock. I have heard so much about it. And the museum has been highly recommended."

"Good. Let's do that. If there's anything else..."

Sharon held up her hand. "I am afraid after this I will need a nap. Would that be possible?"

"Of course. I'll take you home after we're done. Then I'll pick you up again around five thirty. That should give you some time for a good nap."

"That would be wonderful," Sharon said. "I am not used to all this excitement. I find myself rather worn out."

"After Rebecca was born, I started appreciating naps myself. I usually lie down when she does. I'm told as she gets older, she won't want to nap anymore. I'm not sure what I'll do."

"You will do what you have to. That is the way it is when you are a mother."

Cheryl chuckled. "That's certainly true." She stood up. "Let's get going. I'm excited to show you our clock and our incredible museum. You'll love them."

Sharon and Cheryl left the office. Cheryl locked the door behind her. Esther had her own key. Until the thief was caught, Cheryl intended to take every precaution. She didn't want to lose any more merchandise.

She was getting ready to tell Esther and Joni that she and Sharon were leaving when she noticed that Joni looked upset. She followed her gaze and saw Douglas Powell coming in the front door. Joni turned around and headed toward the counter where Cheryl and Sharon stood.

"I think we need to restock our aprons and oven mitts," she said to Cheryl. "Can I go down to the basement and get some?"

"Of course," Cheryl said. "Thank you for noticing." She was pretty sure Esther had just brought some up that morning, but she wasn't going to argue about it. It was clear Joni was bothered by Douglas. Cheryl wondered why. She caught Sharon's eye. "Let's wait a minute before we leave," she whispered.

Sharon, who had noticed Joni's apprehension, nodded.

"Hi, Douglas," Cheryl said with a smile. "Fancy seeing you again. What can we do for you?"

Douglas watched Joni as she opened the basement door and then closed it behind her. "I uh … I thought I'd buy some cookies. Do you have any of those chocolate chip and toffee ones?"

Cheryl gestured to Esther, who was standing a few feet away, watching them. "Can you get Douglas some cookies?" Cheryl asked her.

Esther went to the rack that held cookies. She picked up a package and brought it back to Cheryl at the counter. Cheryl quickly rang up the purchase and put the cookies in a bag. When she held the bag out to Douglas, he didn't take it. He was too busy staring at the basement door.

"Is there anything else?" Cheryl asked.

"Uh…no. I guess not." Douglas hesitated a moment but finally took the bag of cookies and left.

"Okay, what was that about?" Cheryl asked Esther.

"He comes by quite often," Esther said, frowning. "He bothers Joni. Asks her to go out with him. Buys her things. She always gives them back, but Douglas is pushy. He makes us both feel uncomfortable."

The door to the basement slowly opened, and Joni stuck her head out. "Is he gone?" she whispered.

"He's gone," Cheryl said.

Joni closed the basement door and came over to where they waited. "I'm sorry to lie about the aprons," she said. "Douglas makes me nervous. He keeps asking me to have lunch with him or go to the movies."

"He's almost fifteen years older than you," Cheryl said. "That's really inappropriate."

"I know," Joni said. "It's creepy."

"The next time he comes in," Cheryl said, "let me know. I'll have a word with him. Maybe that will stop his harassment."

"The problem is, I know he isn't trying to harass me," Joni said with a sigh. "He just likes me."

Cheryl put her hand on Joni's shoulder. "Joni, a thirty-year-old man shouldn't be asking a sixteen-year-old girl out on a date. He should know better."

"I suppose you're right," she said. "I just hate to hurt his feelings."

"I am not afraid," Esther said. "I would be happy to tell him to buzz off."

Esther, who spent a lot of time with friends who weren't Amish, had picked up quite a few expressions that horrified her parents. Cheryl suspected this was a prime example, and she couldn't help laughing. Hearing "buzz off" from a sweet Amish girl was just too funny. Even Sharon giggled.

"Well, before you tell him that, let me talk to him," Cheryl said, grinning. "Okay?"

Esther nodded slowly. "All right, but he really needs to stop his advances. He is making Joni very uncomfortable. Her boyfriend is really upset about it."

"Who is your boyfriend, Joni?"

The girl blushed. "Warren Pope. We've only been dating about a month."

"And you told him about Douglas?"

"I didn't have to. We were going to the movies. Douglas saw us waiting to get in and came up to talk to me. He said something about going to the movies with him sometime. Right in front of Warren."

Cheryl frowned. That was really odd. "What did Warren say?"

"He didn't say anything. We hadn't been dating very long." Joni pushed a strand of dark hair from her face. "But when Douglas left, Warren asked me about him. I told him just what I told you. That he keeps bothering me. Warren offered to talk to him too, but I said no. I was afraid they might fight. I don't want either one of them to get hurt."

After assuring the girls once again that she would speak to Douglas, Cheryl left the Swiss Miss with Sharon. She didn't want to frighten Joni and Esther, but Douglas's attention disturbed her. Even though he hadn't been charged in connection with Liesel's disappearance, he'd been a suspect. Obviously, there was something about him that had made the police investigate him. Was it possible they'd missed the real perpetrator ten years ago?

CHAPTER THIRTEEN

Sharon enjoyed the quick tour of Sugarcreek Cheryl gave her, especially the Alpine Hills Historical Museum. She found all the exhibits about the village's Swiss and Amish heritage fascinating.

After dropping Sharon off at the cottage, Cheryl headed back to the shop. She'd put her special chicken dish in the Crock-Pot before she left this morning. She needed to add the noodles. They would take two hours to cook. Glancing at her watch, she realized she'd make it home in just enough time to finish the dish. A salad, rolls, and corn would round out the meal nicely. She also wanted to grab a special dessert. One of Naomi's buttermilk pies sounded perfect. She'd noticed a couple of them in the cooler at the shop earlier. Probably, she should have told Esther to hold one for her, but she was sure at least one would still be there when she got back.

She parked her car and got out. As she approached the front door, a young woman came out carrying a large bag. Cheryl smiled at her. She must have purchased several things from the store. Business was pretty good now, even before the festival. After it began, they would have a hard time keeping shelves stocked.

She opened the door and went inside. Esther smiled at her. "I did not expect you back today," she said. "Maam said you were having company for supper."

"She's right. That's why I'm here. I want one of your mother's buttermilk pies for tonight. I noticed two of them when I was here earlier."

"We have not sold any since you left. You should not have a problem. I'll get one for you."

"Thanks, Esther."

Cheryl noticed Joni talking to a customer who was looking over their selection of cookbooks. Amish cookbooks were very popular with tourists. The woman picked two of them from the display and carried them up front. Joni checked her out. She was friendly and professional. Cheryl was happy she had hired Joni. She was a great addition to the store.

The woman walked out of the store, and Cheryl smiled at Joni. "You're doing a great job," she said. "Are you having a good time?"

Joni returned the smile. "I really am. Please don't think my problem with Douglas has ruined things for me. I love working here." She laughed lightly. "I could spend every penny of my wages here. You have such lovely things."

Cheryl chuckled. "Believe me, I understand. I feel the same way."

"Are you waiting for something?" Joni asked. "Can I help?"

"Esther was supposed to be getting me a buttermilk pie. I'm not sure what's taking so long."

Just then, Esther came around the corner with a frown on her face. "I do not understand. The buttermilk pies are gone. I looked in the other coolers, but I was unable to find them. And we don't seem to have as much cheese or sausage as we did earlier. The cooler was full this morning." She looked at Joni. "Did you sell these things?"

Joni shook her head. "I sold a cherry pie earlier and some cheese to one gentleman, but only two blocks. I have no idea—"

Cheryl pointed at some store bags lying on the counter. "Why are these out here?" she asked.

"I was putting them under the counter because we were getting low," Joni said. "But then that lady asked for help with the cookbooks. Sorry. I'll get them off the counter."

"That's not why I'm concerned," Cheryl said. "Did you have any large bags out here?"

Joni nodded and went over to the stack of bags. "I had four of them. Now there's only three. I don't get it."

"I do," Cheryl said. "Call Chief Twitchell. Tell him we've been robbed again." Cheryl ran to the front door, pushed it open, and hurried down the front steps. She jogged out onto the sidewalk and looked up and down the street. She was looking for the young woman she'd passed coming in. She was certain she was the thief they'd been looking for. There was no sign of her. Cheryl thought about running down the street to see if she could catch sight of her, but she decided her time might be better spent giving Chief Twitchell a description. She trudged back in the store, trying not to feel angry at the woman.

When Cheryl came back into the store, Esther looked distraught. "Ach, Cheryl, how could she take things right under our noses? I am so sorry. This is all my fault."

"Of course it's not," Cheryl said soothingly. "This woman has hit several shops in Sugarcreek. No one's caught her. She's very good. I suspect she took a bag when you weren't looking, put what she wanted in it, and timed it to make you think Joni checked her out."

Joni sighed. "I saw a woman with a large bag, but she was walking away from the counter. I thought Esther checked her out."

"Well, she's good, but I got a quick look at her when I came in. I called the chief…"

The door opened, and Chief Twitchell walked in. "She was here?" he asked.

Cheryl nodded. She hurried over to the front door and turned the Open sign to Closed. "I think we need to shut down for a bit." She gestured to Esther and Joni. "Go through the store and try to figure out exactly what she got away with. I can't give you a detailed list until we do inventory, Chief, but at least I can give you a general idea."

"You saw her?" the chief said.

"Yes. I assumed she was a customer." Cheryl sighed. "She was wearing a brown leather coat…"

"Let me guess. Dark brown with silver buttons and embroidered lapels?"

Cheryl's mouth dropped open. "Yes. How did you know? Did you see her too?"

He shook his head. "The coat was stolen from Buttons 'n Bows."

"Oh, my." Cheryl closed her eyes and tried to see the woman in her mind. "She could have been anywhere between sixteen and twenty. Hard to tell. She wore makeup like she was twenty, but her facial features suggested she was younger."

"The drugstore down the street is missin' makeup," the chief said under his breath.

"She had blonde hair, green eyes, I think. Maybe blue." Cheryl sighed. "I had no idea I needed to pay attention to her features. She was pretty. A nice smile." She realized as soon as she said it that the woman's smile had been quick and looked forced. "She had a turned-up nose..."

"What else was she wearin'?"

Cheryl closed her eyes again. "I...I'm just not sure..."

"She wore skinny jeans under her coat with Ugg boots," Joni said. She smiled sheepishly. "I'd love to have a pair of boots like that. It's why I noticed."

"Sounds like the shoes that went missin' the same time as the coat," the chief said.

"Sounds like Gail Murray's lost more than we have," Cheryl said. Gail was a good friend.

"Yeah. Some other things were taken too. A scarf. Some gloves."

Cheryl snorted. "A dark blue knit scarf? Brown leather gloves?"

The chief nodded. "I think that's right. I'd have to check my report."

"She was wearing them." Cheryl shook her head. "What is wrong with this woman? None of us are rich. Theft affects us deeply."

"I've found that most thieves don't care about the people they steal from," Chief Twitchell said. "They think people like you won't miss what they take. Either you're rich and won't miss it, or you have insurance to cover loss."

"What we get from the insurance company rarely covers everything."

"I'm afraid they don't think things out that far. It's selfish. No doubt about it."

Cheryl suddenly remembered the noodles that were supposed to go into her Crock-Pot. She didn't want supper ruined the first night Anton was in town. "Chief, I'm sorry. I need to make a quick phone call. Will you excuse me?"

"I think I'm done here anyway. Thanks for the additional description. It matches Kathy's. This is helpful."

"Aren't you going to dust for fingerprints?" Joni asked.

The chief smiled. "It might be hard to sort out all the fingerprints in here," he said. "And besides, Cheryl mentioned she was wearin' gloves. Wouldn't do much good."

"Oh, yeah. Sorry," Joni said, looking embarrassed.

"Don't be sorry," the chief said. "It was a good idea."

He said goodbye and left.

"Let's stay closed," Cheryl said. "We need to do inventory. I want to know everything she took. Can you both stay and help me?"

"I can," said Esther.

Joni smiled. "Sure."

"Thanks." She sighed. "What kind of desserts do we have left?"

"We have one of those great fudge cakes," Esther said.

Cheryl smiled. "Good. Why don't you ring it up for me? I've got to make a phone call." As Esther went to get the cake, Cheryl took her cell phone out of her pocket. She pulled up her home phone number and clicked on it. A few seconds later, Levi answered.

"Levi, I've been detained at the store. Can you watch Rebecca for a couple more hours?"

"Ja. Is everything all right?"

"No, but I'll tell you what's going on when I get home. I need you to do me another favor." She gave him instructions about how to shred the chicken and find the frozen noodles in the freezer. "Once the chicken is shredded, just dump the noodles in the Crock-Pot, stir it once, and put the lid back on. Make sure the Crock-Pot stays on low."

"All right," he said. "I will take care of it right away."

"Is Anton there yet?" Cheryl asked.

"Ja, he arrived about thirty minutes ago. He is unpacking in the dawdy haus. He wants to take a nap before supper. He will come here around six."

Cheryl could hear something in Levi's voice that concerned her. "Is everything all right?"

Levi sighed. "Ja, I guess so. Anton seems distracted. Not like the person I remember."

"His mother has died, Levi. And his sister has rejected him. Doesn't want him at their mother's funeral. I think that's enough to distract anyone."

"You are right, of course," he said. "I should have thought of that. For some reason I expected him to be my old friend."

"Give him time," Cheryl said gently. "Maybe he'll open up tonight at supper."

"I hope so."

"When I'm done here I'll pick up Sharon and come straight home. Thanks for helping out with Rebecca."

"Rebecca is my daughter too, Cheryl. Watching her is a joy, not a burden."

"Have I ever told you I love you?" Cheryl said, smiling.

"Many, many times."

"Well, here it is again. I love you, Levi."

Levi laughed. "I love you too."

As Cheryl hung up the phone, she could hear Joni and Esther giggling at her profession of love for Levi. She put her phone back in her pocket and turned to smile at them. "You'll both be saying the same thing to your husbands someday. Mark my words."

This made them giggle even harder. Then the three of them set about to do a quick inventory. As she worked, Cheryl had a hard time concentrating. Anton was in Sugarcreek. Would other people in the community react the way the Hostettlers had? Were Levi and Cheryl about to become pariahs in their own hometown?

Chapter Fourteen

After inventory was completed, Cheryl drove over to the cottage to pick up Sharon. Thankfully, the shop was only missing the buttermilk pies, three bags of cookies, two sausages, and three blocks of cheese. Nothing as valuable as the quilt.

Sharon was ready when Cheryl got there. As she drove home, she prayed Levi had taken care of the noodles. If not, supper would be chicken in sauce. Maybe she could make rice and put the chicken over that. She shared her concern with Sharon, who laughed.

"I understand," she said. "My father was a very smart man. He understood crops and animals. He could keep perfect records. His math skills were exceptional. But send him to the store for navy beans, and he would bring back something like pork and beans in a gigantic can. In his mind, beans were beans."

Cheryl giggled. "Not long after we got married, I sent Levi to the store with a short list. Only three items. He brought home a pound of hamburger, two boxes of laundry detergent, and three gallons of bleach."

"Three gallons of bleach? Ach, Cheryl. You must keep a very clean home."

Cheryl grinned at her. "I numbered the list. Number one was hamburger, number two was laundry detergent..."

"And number three was bleach, ain't so?"

The two women laughed heartily. Cheryl really liked Sharon and was so glad she'd come to Sugarcreek. She would miss her when she went home.

"Are you nervous about your guest?" Sharon asked as Cheryl turned on the road that led to their house.

"A little, yes. I mean, I have a lot of confidence in Levi. He feels strongly that Anton isn't anyone we should worry about, but still." She sighed. "I don't mean to be judgmental. But why would some people be so convinced he's guilty? Even if he had nothing to do with Liesel Hostettler's disappearance, there was obviously something about him that made people suspicious. And then I worry a bit about how others will react to us taking him in." She glanced over at Sharon. "I shouldn't care, but I do. And not just because I want to be liked. That's not it. If Liesel's parents truly believe Anton hurt their daughter, then does our involvement send them a message that we don't care about their loss?" She shook her head. "That would really hurt me. The last thing I want to do is add to their pain."

Sharon was silent after Cheryl stopped speaking. Cheryl wondered what she was thinking. She was just about ready to ask when Sharon turned toward her. Cheryl was surprised to see tears in her eyes.

"A few years ago my little cousin Sadie was constantly getting hurt and breaking bones. My aunt and uncle were always at the doctor's office or the emergency room. Someone from the hospital called Social Services and accused my aunt and uncle of abusing

Sadie. They took her out of their home and put her with a foster family. They were not Amish. It was very confusing to Sadie. She really missed her parents, and losing her broke their hearts. Although they told our bishop that they had never hurt Sadie, they were not believed. They were publicly rebuked by our church leaders. I tried to tell people that they would *never* strike her, that they were not abusive. When a social worker noticed the injuries were still occurring, she became suspicious. She contacted a doctor who gave Sadie an exam. The conclusion was that my cousin had Osteogenesis Imperfecta."

Cheryl gasped. "That doesn't sound good. What is it?"

Sharon sighed. "It's an awful diagnosis, more commonly known as brittle bone disease. The entire time, Sadie had a condition that caused her bones to break easily. Her parents were not abusing her."

"So what happened?" Cheryl asked.

"Sadie was sent home with a list of instructions for them to carry out. Ways to keep her safe." Sharon sighed and looked out the window. A few seconds later, she turned back. "The elders apologized, but my aunt and uncle were never the same. It was as if something inside them had broken. Sometimes we can have the best intentions, but if we don't have the truth, people can be hurt. If only people had believed the best about them..." She smiled. "Not the people from social services. The pain was caused by the people who knew them."

Cheryl rolled Sharon's comments over in her mind. She was right. Then another Scripture whispered to her. The one where

Jesus warned His disciples to be as wise as serpents and as harmless as doves. What was wisdom in this situation with Anton? Cheryl planned to give him the benefit of the doubt, but at the same time, she planned to keep a close watch on him. She thought about Douglas. Did she need to be careful about jumping to conclusions about him as well? Or was knowing a thirty-year-old man was asking out a sixteen-year-old girl enough to raise suspicions? Cheryl decided she would make certain Joni told her parents about Douglas. It was really their business to know about the situation.

Before turning in to their driveway, Cheryl stopped at the mailbox and got the mail. She was happy to see an envelope she recognized. A letter from Aunt Mitzi. Cheryl missed her so much. She understood her aunt's decision to go back to her mission work in Papua New Guinea, but her recent stay in Sugarcreek had made it hard to say goodbye again.

There was a red sports car parked on one side of the driveway. Anton really had shed his Amish roots. Cheryl and Sharon got out of the truck. Cheryl put the mail in her coat pocket so she could safely carry the fudge cake. The last thing she wanted to do was drop it on the ground. Except for some old ice cream in the freezer, there weren't any other desserts in the house appropriate for company.

As she and Sharon approached the front door, it swung open. Levi stood there with Rebecca in his arms. When she saw Cheryl, she laughed and held her arms out.

"I see my popularity just dropped," Levi said, laughing.

"I can't hold you yet, Boo Bear," Cheryl said, smiling at her daughter. "Let me put the cake down, and I'll be glad to snuggle."

"So glad you could join us this evening," Levi said to Sharon.

"Thank you for allowing me to share supper with you," she said, smiling. "Something smells wonderful."

Cheryl went into the kitchen, put the cake on the counter, and checked the Crock-Pot. Sure enough, Levi had put the noodles in. It was almost done. Cheryl grabbed a big spoon and stirred the mixture. It smelled great and was one of Cheryl's best dishes. She wasn't the cook Naomi was, but she was getting better with her mother-in-law's help and good recipes like this one.

She went back into the living room and took Rebecca from Levi. She hugged her and cuddled with her for a few minutes before going back into the kitchen to prepare supper. She put some fresh corn on the stove and made up a salad. Then she put rolls in the oven. With her chocolate cake for dessert, she felt she'd put together a nice meal for Anton's first night in Sugarcreek.

"Can I do something to help?"

Cheryl turned around to find Sharon standing in the doorway.

"I feel useless just sitting in the living room, although playing with Rebecca is very enjoyable."

Cheryl smiled at her. "If you want to set the table, that would be very helpful."

Cheryl showed Sharon where she kept the silverware, the plates, and the glasses. As Sharon set the table, Cheryl dipped the chicken and noodles out of the Crock-Pot and into a large serving bowl. Then she put the salad on the table along with salad bowls.

As she checked the corn, she glanced out the kitchen window. A man was coming out of the dawdy haus. He closed the door behind him, paused, and then turned and began walking toward the house.

He was tall with dark hair. Quite handsome. Cheryl's stomach tightened. There was no going back now. Anton Birken was here. From this moment forward, things in Sugarcreek were going to get interesting.

Chapter Fifteen

Even though she expected Anton's knock on her front door, Cheryl still jumped when it happened. She took the corn off the stove, transferred it to a serving bowl, and checked on the rolls. They were almost done. Cheryl turned the heat down so they wouldn't burn. Then she took a deep breath and headed toward the living room. Sharon came with her but didn't say anything until she was introduced to Anton.

"This is my friend, Anton Birken," Levi said with a big smile. He clapped Anton on the back and grinned at Cheryl.

"Anton, this is my beautiful wife, Cheryl."

"I'm pleased to meet you," Cheryl said, extending her hand. Anton took her hand and shook it. "This is our guest, Sharon Vogel," she said, gesturing toward Sharon.

"I am happy to meet you," Sharon said.

Anton's gaze traveled up and down Sharon's conservative dress. His rather guarded expression became even more distant. His lips thinned.

"I assure you, Mr. Birken," Sharon said, "I am not a representative from the Sugarcreek Amish community. I am in town from Pennsylvania to do business with Cheryl's shop. You are safe with me."

Sharon's playful smile caused Anton to laugh. "I'm sorry," he said. "I didn't mean to be rude."

"You were not rude," Sharon said. "You were a little suspicious, but you have no problem with me. Besides, I am staying in Cheryl's cottage. There is electricity, and I confess that I am enjoying it. Now that my secret is out, perhaps you can relax around me."

"I have a feeling relaxing around you would be a mistake. You're too sharp for that."

His comment made Cheryl smile. So far, she liked him. Hopefully, it would make for a pleasant evening.

"Please make yourself comfortable," she said, gesturing to the couch and chairs in the living room. "Supper is almost ready."

"Something smells wonderful," Anton said. Up close, he really was very handsome. Deep blue eyes and dark wavy hair. His manner certainly didn't make him seem like a dangerous person. Instead, Cheryl found him quite charming.

"Can I get you something to drink?" Cheryl asked. "Coffee? Tea?"

"I can wait for supper," Anton said. He sat down in a chair. Levi sat down on the couch next to Rebecca, who seemed focused on her toys and not their visitors.

"Cheryl, I'm sure there is something else I can do," Sharon said.

Cheryl started to tell her she didn't need further help, but then she noticed a pleading look in Sharon's eyes.

"Sure. Thanks, Sharon," she said.

She'd turned toward the kitchen when suddenly Rebecca ran toward Anton, who put his arms out. When Rebecca reached him, he scooped her up and swung her up over his head. Rebecca squealed with laughter.

Cheryl immediately tensed up and started to tell Anton to put her down. Before she had a chance to say anything, Sharon took her by the arm and gently led her away. When they reached the kitchen, Cheryl pulled her arm away.

"Why did you do that?" she asked under her breath.

"Because you were getting ready to say something I think you would regret," Sharon said in a low voice. "If it had been anyone else, would you have rebuked them for playing with Rebecca?"

Cheryl bit her lip as she considered Sharon's question. What would she have said if Sharon hadn't stopped her? The words on the tip of her tongue were "Put her down!" She shook her head at the realization. "I'm sure you're right," she told Sharon. "But that's my baby."

"Levi is with her. He would not let harm come to her. Besides, if Anton is an innocent man..."

"Then I would have offended him." Cheryl folded her arms across her chest. "This is harder than I thought."

"Then you can understand the reaction of others toward Mr. Birken."

"Yes." Cheryl steadied herself by remembering what Sharon had pointed out. That Levi was with Rebecca. He would never allow anyone to hurt her. Cheryl was ashamed of what she almost said, but her reaction when she thought of Rebecca's safety was almost instinct. Something she couldn't control.

Cheryl forced herself to finish getting supper ready. With Sharon's help, a few minutes later, everything was on the table. She called everyone in to eat. Levi put Rebecca into her high chair while Sharon and Cheryl got drinks.

When they were all gathered around the table, Cheryl realized they had a small problem. Levi prayed out loud now since it was the way Cheryl was used to.

"Please, pray the way you are used to," Sharon said. "I am not that fragile."

Cheryl smiled at her. "Thank you. We don't want to do anything to offend you. We understand and love the Amish ways."

"I know that, and I thank you," Sharon said with a smile.

Cheryl and Levi bowed their heads. Even little Rebecca put her hands together. Levi blessed the food and prayed that God would bless their guests. Cheryl snuck a look at Anton while Levi prayed. His eyes stayed open even though his head was bowed. Had he just turned his back on his Amish roots? Or had he dismissed God completely from his life? Cheryl silently prayed that if that were true, God would touch his heart and lead him back.

When Levi said, "Amen," Rebecca clapped enthusiastically and everyone looked up. Levi started the bowl of chicken and noodles around the table.

"I wanted to tell you how sorry we are about your mother," Cheryl said to Anton. "I didn't know her, but I've heard very nice things about her."

"She was a wonderful woman," Anton said. "She deserved better than she got."

"You never spoke to her again after you left?" Levi asked.

"No. I didn't feel free to come back here. It would have been too hard on her. I sent her several letters, but she never responded. I hope she read them. I have no way of knowing."

"Maybe your sister can tell you about that," Cheryl said.

Anton shrugged. "My sister may have kept my letters from my mother. I hope I'm wrong, but Meredith was very angry when I left. A lot of people in Sugarcreek were convinced I had something to do with that poor girl's disappearance." He sighed as he spooned corn onto his plate. "We were friends. That was it. I had no romantic feelings toward her. Douglas Powell was the one who had a crush on her. I told Chief Twitchell about him, but it seemed that Douglas had an alibi."

"Why did so many people think you were involved?" Cheryl asked.

Levi tried to shush her, but Anton shook his head. "It's okay. She can ask. There's nothing I won't discuss with you." He put his fork down and leaned back in his chair. "Liesel was a nice girl but unhappy with her life. She and I were kindred spirits. We both had dreams that didn't look as if they'd come true if we stayed in the Amish church. We talked quite a bit. Liesel made plans to run away . . . someday." He shook his head. "I didn't think she was serious. I was certain it was just a childish threat. But then one day she was just . . . gone. She didn't tell me she was leaving. To this day I have no idea what happened to her."

"Chief Twitchell told us there was a note?" Cheryl said.

"Yes," Anton said. "That note was the nail in my coffin as far as the community was concerned. Her parents found it after she went missing. It was supposed to be from me, asking her to meet me at the Noffsinger house that last night. It was typed. It's true I spent some time on the computer at the library, but I was just looking things up. Trying to find out about other places in the world. I was curious. But I never typed anything out. Ever."

"It's odd," Cheryl said. "If someone was trying to make you look guilty, that was the way to do it. Type out the note so no one could prove you didn't send it."

Anton nodded. "It's very troubling, and it's bothered me all these years." He leaned forward again and picked up his fork. "I really hope Liesel did run away. It's better than the alternative."

"Her parents must be heartbroken," Sharon said softly. "Sometimes it feels better to blame someone else for a loss than to look inward. Perhaps her unhappiness led her to leave on her own and start a new life somewhere else."

"And not let her parents know she was okay?" Cheryl said. She reached over and patted Rebecca's cheek. She couldn't imagine the pain it would cause a parent to not know what had happened to their child.

"That's always bothered me," Anton said. "Liesel would have left a note—tried to explain to her parents why she left."

"But I have seen it before," Sharon said. "The children convince themselves they will be shunned anyway. They believe there is no reason to contact their parents." She shook her head. "This reasoning has caused hurt. No matter what happens down the road, parents love their children. They want to know they are safe."

Anton was strangely silent during Sharon's comments. Cheryl wondered what he was thinking. He looked up suddenly, and his eyes met hers. He smiled sadly.

"I guess sending letters wasn't enough," he said, looking down at his plate. "My sister doesn't want me here, and my mother never reached out to me. Was I wrong to come here?"

Cheryl just stared at him. She honestly didn't know what to tell him.

CHAPTER SIXTEEN

Levi and Sharon both seemed to feel Anton had done the right thing returning to Sugarcreek for his mother's funeral. They offered him encouragement and by the time they'd finished, he seemed to feel better. But Cheryl wasn't convinced. After all, his mother was gone. It wasn't helping her. And his sister needed to mourn the loss of her mother, not worry about a brother she didn't want at the funeral. Wouldn't it have been kinder to stay away? Cheryl wasn't certain. She couldn't imagine losing her parents. Even though her brother had distanced himself from the family for a while, eventually he felt the need to reconnect. They were all very close now. Family members should never reject each other. It was the nature of family. No matter what mistakes you made, your family should always support you. Love you anyway. Even though Levi had left the Amish church, he was still close to his parents, brothers, and sisters.

After supper, Cheryl drove Sharon home, then came back, and got Rebecca ready for bed. Levi walked Anton back to the dawdy haus.

Cheryl found herself feeling sorry for Anton. He seemed to be a good man who'd loved his mother. Cheryl wondered why she'd never responded to his letters. Was it because she considered him shunned? Or could he be right about suspecting his sister made sure she never got them? A darker thought kept trying to find a place in her mind. Was it because she and her daughter knew something about Anton that others only suspected?

Cheryl felt a frisson of fear slither around inside her. As she waited for Levi to return, she prayed for God's wisdom and protection.

About fifteen minutes later, Levi came in the back door. Cheryl was waiting for him in the living room. Rebecca had fallen asleep in her arms as she rocked her and sang one of Rebecca's favorite songs, "Hushabye Mountain."

He smiled when he saw his wife and daughter. "I am glad you waited for me. We can put Rebecca in bed together." He reached down and took his sleeping daughter from Cheryl's arms. He carried her into her bedroom and put her in her crib. Levi reached for Cheryl's hand as she whispered a prayer. They stood there for a few minutes, just watching their daughter sleep. Her sweetness was almost overwhelming. When he was a baby, did Anton's mother watch him sleep? Did she feel as blessed as Cheryl and Levi felt right now? A tear slipped down Cheryl's cheek. Having Anton here was bringing up all kinds of emotions she hadn't anticipated.

Levi took her by the arm and led her out of Rebecca's bedroom. When they reached the living room, he asked, "Are you all right? You seem upset."

Cheryl shook her head as she walked into the kitchen to clean up from supper. Levi followed her. "Anton's story confuses me," she said. "Liesel Hostettler's disappearance seems to have devastated two families. I can't understand how a mother can turn against her child. Believe him to be…evil. What did he do to evoke that kind of response? And if Liesel is alive, living another life somewhere, how could she do that to her parents? I look at Rebecca and wonder if someday she'll want to live a life without us." She wiped her eyes and met Levi's gaze. "It scares me."

Levi took her hands in his. "Oh, Cheryl. You see these two examples but you forget all the others. Look at my family. Two of the children have left the Amish faith, yet our bond is stronger than ever. And what about your family? You have had your problems, but you and your parents and your brother found a way to stay close. Anton and Liesel are not the standard. They are the exception. Besides, it is possible Liesel is not alive. Certainly not by Anton's hand, but we would be naive to not consider the possibility."

"That makes it even worse, doesn't it?" Cheryl asked.

Levi sighed. "For her parents? They either believe she loved them so little she ran away and did not ever get in touch with them—or that someone else made it impossible for her to contact them." He shook his head. "Both options are terrible."

"Yes, they are." Cheryl kissed his cheek and turned around to start washing the dishes. Levi came up beside her. "Let me help you." Twenty minutes later, they were done and headed to bed. As Cheryl turned out the light in the kitchen, she noticed Anton sitting on the front porch of the dawdy haus. Was he thinking some of the same things Cheryl was? She prayed they both would get some sleep tonight.

Thankfully, Cheryl fell asleep as soon as her head hit the pillow. She felt Levi get up a couple of times and wondered why he was restless, but she was so tired, she just went back to sleep.

Thursday morning, Cheryl awoke to the sound of rain. Except for Levi's soft snoring, the house was silent. Rebecca was still asleep. Although Cheryl felt like staying underneath the covers, she realized she could have some quiet time to herself. She swung her legs over the side of the bed and sat there a moment, trying to wake up completely. Then she quietly got out of bed, found her robe, and went out into the kitchen. She made coffee and whipped up some waffle mix. Rebecca and Levi loved waffles.

She poured herself a cup of coffee and sat down at the kitchen table, looking out the window at the rain. Their cows and sheep were out in the corral, waiting for breakfast. Their horses were still in the barn, obviously not fond of getting wet. Cheryl had been trying to find some time to ride her horse, Ranger, but it seemed something kept coming up. Either it was too cold, or it was raining. If she didn't find time soon, it could be a while. Winter was on the way.

"Getting some time alone before the day starts?"

Cheryl turned her head to see Levi walk into the room.

"Yeah, something like that."

"You need to spend some time with Ranger," he said as he headed for the coffeemaker. "It has been too long."

"How do you do that?" Cheryl asked with a smile. "Read my mind like that?"

He smiled as he poured himself a cup of coffee. "We are too alike, you and I. I know how much you love your horse and how much riding relaxes you. It will be cold soon. You should go before the temperatures drop."

"I agree." She took a sip of coffee. "Maybe after Anton leaves."

Levi sat down at the table. "Are you feeling better about his visit?"

Cheryl sighed. "I still have some concerns, but I trust your judgment. You have good intuition when it comes to people." She frowned at him. "I felt you get up a couple of times during the night," she said. "Are you feeling okay?"

He nodded. "I just had a hard time sleeping." He sighed and ran his hand through his blond hair. "I trust Anton, I really do. But now that he is here..." He sought her eyes. "I wonder if I should have put him so close to my family."

"Look, he's here now. We can't keep changing our minds about him. I think we need to trust your original instincts. You were so sure of his innocence."

"I am sure..." He leaned back in his chair and sighed again. This time it seemed to come from somewhere deep inside. "I did not want him to think I suspected him in Liesel's disappearance, but..." He shook his head. "Being a father and a husband brings up feelings and thoughts I am not used to. Feelings of protection. An almost overwhelming desire to keep my family safe. It is beyond reason. My response to Anton was thought out very carefully, and I was happy with the conclusion I reached. But now..."

Cheryl giggled. "If I didn't know better, I'd say you were hormonal."

Levi's eyes widened in surprise. "Hormonal? I do not think..."

"Don't get upset," she said with a smile. "When I was pregnant, I felt so...so protective of the little life inside me. It was stronger than anything I anticipated. And it was, as you said, beyond reason. I chalked it up to hormones, but maybe I was wrong. Maybe it was the realization that I was responsible for a human being. A child. My body seemed to understand more than my brain did." She wrapped her arms around herself. The morning was chilly, and she hadn't turned the heat up yet. "I believe God gives us an instinct to protect our children, Levi. What you're feeling is perfectly normal." Although she didn't tell Levi about her reaction when Anton picked up Rebecca, she understood it now.

Levi took another sip of coffee, and then he set his cup down. "I guess so, but it is certainly unsettling." He reached over and took her hand. "I would never put you and Rebecca in danger on purpose. Never."

"I know that."

A low cry from the other room made it clear Rebecca was awake. Cheryl started to get up, but Levi leaned over and gently pushed her back down. "I will get her. You finish your coffee."

Cheryl put her hand over his. "I knew I loved you for some reason."

He leaned down and kissed the top of her head. "I love you for many, many reasons."

He left the room to get Rebecca, who would need a diaper change and an outfit for the day. Cheryl considered following Levi to make sure he picked the right clothes for her, but she talked herself out of it. If his choice wasn't appropriate, she'd change Rebecca when he went out to feed their livestock.

She felt something soft rub against her leg and looked down to see Beau, who was letting her know he wanted to be fed too. She reached down and stroked his soft fur. "Good morning. You decided to get up too, huh?"

She rose from the table, filled his food and water bowls. She heard Levi laughing from the other room as Rebecca cooed. She got out her waffle iron and began to make waffles. She also took out a frying pan and put on some bacon. Within a few minutes, it was sizzling. When Levi brought Rebecca in, she was dressed in her pink overalls with the lace edging. One of her very cutest outfits. Her little feet were clad in white shoes with pink lacy socks.

"She looks great," Cheryl said with a smile.

"So you will not re-dress her when I leave?" he asked. "I notice when you do that."

Cheryl laughed. "No, I won't re-dress her."

As Levi put Rebecca in her high chair, Beau came over and stood up on his back feet, trying to stretch himself so Rebecca could pet him. Levi laughed and sat down next to her.

Cheryl took a moment to look at her family and thank God for the incredible life He'd given her.

"I told you we could eat cereal," Levi said, seeing the waffle maker.

"It's cold and wet out. I don't want you out there with cold cereal in your stomach."

"Ach, Cheryl," he said, grinning, "I think food warms up when it gets into your stomach."

She waved her spatula at him. "Maybe so, but this breakfast will go down warm. Just hush up."

Levi turned to Rebecca. "Do you hear the way your mother speaks to me? She tells me to hush up. What do you think of that, Boo?"

Rebecca reached out and grabbed Levi's arm. "Dada, Dada, Dada," she said.

"She agrees with me," Cheryl said.

"How do you get that from Dada, Dada, Dada?" Levi asked with a frown.

"I speak baby. I know what she means."

"Oh, I see." He made a face, and Rebecca laughed again.

A few minutes later, Cheryl put plates on the table with waffles and bacon. She warmed up the maple syrup in the microwave and also placed it on the table along with the butter. Rebecca got a small plate with some cut-up waffle and a cup of juice.

After they ate, Levi put on his coat and went out to feed the animals and check their fields. Next month they would take their fall crop to auction in Holmes County. Cheryl prayed the weather wouldn't get any colder. They needed the money from the auction to make it through the winter. Levi's parents also relied heavily on the auction. Thankfully, both families had other sources of income to help them between harvests. The Millers had their corn maze and their petting zoo, and of course, sales from the Swiss Miss came in handy for Cheryl and Levi. The festival at the end of the month brought in many visitors, and sales were usually brisk. Cheryl felt they would do well this year. That would help both families.

Cheryl sighed happily as Rebecca sang in her high chair. She sang a lot. Cheryl and Levi had no idea what she was singing about, but it seemed to make sense to her. Rebecca actually had a nice voice for a baby. Most of the time she sang on key when she tried to repeat some of the songs Cheryl shared with her at night before bed.

A few minutes later, Levi came back into the house. "I forgot my gloves," he said. "I must be distracted."

His restlessness last night, along with the feeling he was worried about something this morning, made Cheryl ask, "Levi, has something happened to upset you?"

He stopped and stared at her for a moment before saying, "Last night Anton left for a while. He was gone over an hour." Levi frowned at her. "Where could he have gone, Cheryl?"

CHAPTER SEVENTEEN

A fter getting his gloves, Levi went back outside. As Cheryl cleaned up the kitchen, she tried to put concerns about Anton out of her mind. Levi was overreacting. Maybe Anton needed something from the pharmacy, or maybe he just wanted to drive around Sugarcreek. After all, it had been years since he'd been there.

Cheryl had thought about calling Anton to see if he wanted breakfast, but he'd made it clear last night that he planned on feeding himself. He had no desire to cause Cheryl and Levi additional work. Still, Cheryl had invited him to eat supper with them, at least, while he was there. He'd finally agreed, "If you're sure it's not an inconvenience," he'd said.

"Hardly," Cheryl had replied. "I'm making supper anyway, and I always make too much." She'd smiled at him. "Fear of not having enough, I guess."

"Well, that works out great for me," he'd said. "Your chicken and noodles are the best I've ever had. And that's saying a lot. Growing up Amish, I've eaten a lot of great food."

Cheryl had laughed. She knew just what he meant. Amish women prided themselves on their cooking. She'd blushed at Anton's comment.

"Thank you," she'd said, her cheeks feeling warm. "That recipe was Naomi's. I adjusted it for the Crock-Pot."

"That might be so," he'd said. "But you prepared it, and it was absolutely wonderful."

"Thank you, Anton," she'd said. "Cooking for someone like you is a pleasure."

Remembering the time she'd spent with Anton gave her a real sense of peace. He really was a nice man. She didn't sense anything in him that gave her concern.

As Cheryl put the dishes away, Rebecca entertained herself on the living room floor with some of her toys. When she was done, Cheryl got out the letter Aunt Mitzi had sent her. When she opened it, some pictures fell out. Cheryl picked them up. They were pictures of Aunt Mitzi with some of the local people she worked with in Papua New Guinea. They appeared to be standing in front of the health clinic Mitzi had helped establish for the community. Cheryl looked at the next picture and laughed. It was Aunt Mitzi and her goat friend, Georgie. Georgie had been adopted by Mitzi and her missionary friends. Named after Cheryl's father, Mitzi's brother, the little goat had gone from being a stray to becoming a valued and loved member of the group. If goats could smile, Georgie was smiling.

Cheryl put the pictures on the table next to her and opened the letter.

My beautiful Cheryl,

Everything is going well here. We had almost two hundred people in church last Sunday. The clinic is always busy, and we have several new doctors who have offered to volunteer their time to help our friends. Even though I rejoice in seeing God's hand in our efforts, I think of you often and miss you.

For now, it is God's will for us to be apart, but I hope someday, on this side of heaven, we will be together again.

We had a little drama here last week. A local man was accused of stealing his neighbor's milk cow. Although most of the community, even some in our church, believed this man to be guilty, he insisted he didn't have the cow. Sure enough, the poor creature was found two miles away, wandering in a field. She'd found a broken place in the fence that surrounded the owner's property and decided to do a little exploring.

It was a lesson in "believing the best" and not convicting people when we don't have the facts. If only we all understood what love is: *"Love is patient, love is kind. It does not envy, it does not boast, it is not proud. It does not dishonor others, it is not self-seeking, it is not easily angered, it keeps no record of wrongs. Love does not delight in evil but rejoices with the truth. It always protects, always trusts, always hopes, always perseveres."*

Although it is true that we must be wise, only God can look on the heart. When we judge others, we cannot do it without the Holy Spirit who knows all things. If He does not warn us or show us that we need to distrust another human being, our job is to offer support. Belief. And trust.

I hope our community has learned an important lesson from this experience.

Well, I'd better wrap this up. I hear someone calling my name. It's time for lunch. When you write next time, I'd love to see some current pictures of Rebecca. I'm sure she's getting big! Give her a big hug and kiss from Aunt Mitzi!

My love to you, Levi, and my little Boo Bear.

Mit*zi*

Cheryl folded the letter and slid it back into the envelope. Then she added the pictures. How did Mitzi do it? It was as if she were watching them. Knew exactly what was going on. Her letter couldn't have come at a better time. Cheryl had to stop worrying about Anton. Give the situation to God. If there was something to be concerned about, He would have to tell them. Until then, it was their job to love Anton. To believe the best about him.

Her thoughts drifted to Douglas and immediately her stomach clenched. Was that the Holy Spirit warning her? She certainly had a different reaction to him than she did to Anton.

"God, I'm tired of being afraid of Anton," she prayed softly. "If there's something wrong with him, will You let us know? Or just make him leave town. Otherwise, I'm going to show him Christian love and acceptance—something I think he needs right now. As far as Douglas goes…" She thought for a moment. "Will You show me what to do? Unless You tell me not to, I intend to talk to him. I want to be kind. Not assume the worst. But I also need to be firm. He needs to leave Joni alone. I would appreciate Your help with this. Thank You, Lord."

She felt a burden lift as she prayed. Rebecca squealed at one of her toys, making Cheryl laugh. Rebecca had a way of enjoying every toy as if she'd never seen it before. If only adults could view each new day with such joy.

"I need to be more like you," she told Rebecca. "Except for spitting out food I don't like. Other people might not understand."

Although Rebecca had no idea what her mother was talking about, she laughed as if she did.

Today, Cheryl and Levi were taking Anton and Sharon to lunch at Yoder's Corner. Sharon planned to go home on Saturday. Cheryl realized she would miss her. Anton was only staying until after the funeral tomorrow. After some of the things he'd said, she wondered if he'd been rethinking his decision to attend. Levi planned for all of them to go together. Cheryl had been a little concerned about walking into the service with Anton, but she was serious about believing the best. She and Levi would just have to keep their chins up and pray others at the funeral would understand. Cheryl had seen the love and forgiveness extended by the Amish community and trusted they would come through again.

Last night on the way home Sharon had offered to stay with Rebecca while they attended the funeral, and Cheryl had agreed. Rebecca really seemed to like her, and Cheryl didn't think taking a toddler to an Amish funeral was a good idea. It was a serious and very staid experience.

Cheryl had just put Mitzi's letter away when Levi came back into the house.

"I'd like to run to the shop for a while before lunch," she told him. "Can I meet you, Rebecca, and Anton at the restaurant? I just want to make sure we're getting everything in we need for the festival. Esther's doing a great job, but preparing for the festival is a huge undertaking. I don't want her to feel overwhelmed."

Levi nodded. "I want to run over to check on our corn maze, but I'll just take Rebecca with me. Elizabeth will be there and can keep her entertained. The maze needs to be in perfect shape for the festival, and Eli has requested my help. I'll meet you at Yoder's."

"You're a very handy fellow," Cheryl said, winking at Levi. "I believe I'll keep you."

"I am quite relieved to hear that."

Cheryl went into the bedroom and got dressed for town. Before she left, she called the shop and Esther answered.

"I'm coming by this morning," she told her. "Just want to make sure our ducks are all in a row for the festival."

"All right," Esther said. "Almost everything is here. I am still waiting on a few of our sellers to get their goods in, but I am not overly concerned about any of them."

Although Esther's message was positive, Cheryl could hear something in her voice that concerned her. "Is everything okay?" she asked.

"Ja. I am sorry, Cheryl. Douglas has driven by the store several times since Joni arrived. It is making us both uncomfortable."

"Call Chief Twitchell," Cheryl said. "Tell him about it. He can put a stop to it."

"Joni will not allow me to do that," Esther said.

Cheryl was surprised. "Why?"

"She is afraid her boyfriend will find out and get angry. It seems they had a disagreement about Douglas." Esther's voice was almost a whisper.

"Well, I'm not afraid of her boyfriend," Cheryl said. "I'll call the chief."

There was only silence. Finally, Esther said, "Perhaps you could talk to Joni first?"

"No, Esther," Cheryl said. Her distrust of Douglas made her even more concerned about his actions. "Put Joni in my office and lock the door. I'm calling the chief right now."

Cheryl hung up and quickly called the police station. As she waited for the chief to come on the line, she began to wonder about Liesel. Had Douglas stalked her too before she disappeared?

CHAPTER EIGHTEEN

After telling Levi what was going on, Cheryl headed over to the Swiss Miss. Chief Twitchell had promised to talk to Joni. If she lodged a complaint, he said he'd look for Douglas and warn him to stay away from her. Since he hadn't done anything wrong, the chief couldn't arrest him.

Cheryl felt frustrated. She understood that the police couldn't do much about someone's intentions, but Douglas's presence was concerning. He needed to stop. Would a warning from the chief put an end to his unwanted attention?

As she headed for the shop, she wondered what she should say to Joni. Why was she hesitant to tell the police about Douglas? Because her boyfriend was jealous? That didn't make sense. It was childish and ill advised. She didn't want to upset Joni, but she couldn't stand by and allow this to continue. Liesel's disappearance made the situation even more serious. She didn't plan to wait until Joni went missing too.

As she parked in front of the Swiss Miss, she noticed the chief's car already there. She hurried inside, hoping everything was okay. When she opened the door, she saw Esther and Joni talking to the chief. Joni was crying. Esther had her arm around the distressed girl.

Cheryl turned the Open sign to Closed and locked the door. She didn't want to risk having someone come in and find her staff in tears.

The chief greeted her. "Been tryin' to talk to this young lady, but she doesn't seem to want to tell me about her problem."

"Joni, if Douglas Powell is bothering you, you need to tell the chief. He's not going to arrest him, but he will talk to him. A thirty-year-old man shouldn't be approaching a girl your age. We've already been over this."

Joni scowled. "But I don't need the police. I'll just tell him to leave me alone."

"Have you tried to talk to him?" Cheryl asked.

Joni looked down at the floor. "N-no. I mean, I will."

Cheryl sighed. "Joni, you need to be honest with us. Are you afraid to tell him to back off? I can go with you. Would that help?"

Joni took a deep, shuddering breath. "No. No, I'll do it."

Cheryl felt that Joni's declaration was at the very least insincere. She looked at Esther for help. She knew the situation had something to do with Warren Pope, but she didn't want to betray Esther's confidence.

"She is afraid her boyfriend will get into an altercation with Douglas," Esther blurted out.

"Esther!" Joni exclaimed. "I told you that in private."

Esther shook her head. "I am sorry, Joni, but this must stop. You should not be so afraid. Maybe the chief should talk to Douglas and to Warren as well."

"No!" Joni's look of horror surprised Cheryl.

She went over and took the girl's hands. "Joni, are you really that concerned that Warren and Douglas will fight each other?"

Joni sobbed. "Warren gets...angry. I'm afraid something will happen to him. I love him. I really do."

Although Cheryl was pretty sure that at sixteen, Joni didn't know what lasting love was, she didn't say anything. Just reached over and hugged her.

"Look," the chief said to Cheryl. "Unless she files a complaint, I can't do much, but I will definitely have a word with Douglas."

Joni started to say something but the chief raised his hand like a cop stopping traffic. "No, young lady. You don't get to tell me what I can and can't do. No man his age should be askin' a teenager out on a date. Period. Douglas can't get mad at your boyfriend if I approach him. He can only get mad at me, and I don't think he wants to take me on."

Joni seemed to consider this. "But Douglas will know I said something to you."

The chief snorted. "Tough. I'm sure he knows he's upsettin' you, but he hasn't taken the hint. Talkin' to me is the next step. I'm pretty sure this will end your problem." He shook a finger at her. "But if he comes around again, I expect you to call me. You understand?"

Joni nodded slowly. The tension in her face eased some.

"Once the chief talks to him," Cheryl said, "things will get better, okay?"

Joni gave her a small, unsteady smile. "You might be right," she said. She looked at Chief Twitchell. "Thank you," she said softly. "I'm sorry I've been such a pain."

The chief smiled back at her. "You're not a pain. This is my job. Just doin' it the best I can."

"Thanks," said Joni.

"I best be goin'," the chief said to Cheryl. "If you need anything else…"

"I'll call you," Cheryl said. "Thanks, Chief."

He tipped his hat and headed for the front door. Cheryl ran ahead of him and unlocked it. Then she turned the Closed sign over to Open.

"Now, let's go through everything to make sure we're ready for the festival," Cheryl told the girls. "I have a list in my office of the goods we're supposed to have before the festival begins. I want to know what's in and what isn't. And we need to make sure we're fully staffed."

"We have received quite a few things," Esther said, "but Mrs. Bakker still hasn't brought by those aprons and oven mitts."

"Let's give her a call and check on them," Cheryl said. "She usually runs a little behind. I'm sure we'll have them in time."

The phone rang, and Esther answered it. She asked the caller to wait and smiled at Cheryl. "It is Levi," she said.

Cheryl picked up the phone. "Cheryl, Anton would like to see the shop," Levi said. "Why don't we come by there first before we go to lunch?"

"That would be fine," she said, "but I still have to pick up Sharon."

"I totally forgot about that. We can go to the shop after lunch if you would rather."

"Why don't we do that?" Cheryl said. "I think it would make it easier."

"All right. We will meet you at Yoder's at noon."

Cheryl said goodbye and hung up. Having two guests in town right before the Swiss Festival was challenging, but if they both left by Saturday as planned, everything would work out all right. All Cheryl had to do was hang on for a few more days.

After going over a few other things with Esther and Joni, Cheryl drove to the cottage to get Sharon. She was waiting for her on the porch and came down to the car when Cheryl pulled into the driveway.

"*Goot* morning," Sharon said as she got into the car. "I had such a nice sleep last night. The bed is so comfortable."

"I'm glad," Cheryl said with a smile. "I'm happy you came to Sugarcreek and that we got to know each other. I'm also thrilled we'll be doing business together. I'll certainly miss you when you leave. Levi and I will drive you to the bus station Saturday morning."

"Cheryl, would it be possible for me to stay a little longer? I am having such a nice time here."

"I'm sure we can work something out, Sharon," Cheryl said. "It's not hard to change a bus ticket."

Sharon didn't respond. She just nodded. Cheryl was a little surprised. Then a vision of Sharon staring at Anton popped into her head. Her demeanor was different when she was around him. Surely, she didn't want to stay because of Anton. Cheryl sighed inwardly. Anton was kind to Sharon, but Cheryl wasn't sure he'd shown any interest in her romantically. Changing Sharon's travel plans might be simple, but mending a broken heart would be a lot harder.

Chapter Nineteen

Cheryl wanted to talk to Sharon about Anton and find the right words to help her consider if her feelings were misplaced, but there wasn't time. Within minutes, they pulled up in front of one of Sugarcreek's most popular restaurants, Yoder's Corner. Run by Greta and August Yoder, it was known for its homemade dishes. Most of the servers were Amish, and the personality of Sugarcreek was reflected in their food, including many German and Swiss dishes, homemade sausage and sauerkraut, and wonderful desserts. And they served Yoder's Trail Bologna, which was made not far from Sugarcreek. It was unlike any bologna Cheryl had ever tasted.

Cheryl saw Levi's truck in the parking lot. As she and Sharon headed into the restaurant, Cheryl's head was spinning. What could she do about Sharon? She was certain Anton didn't feel the same way about her, and he'd made it clear he wasn't interested in being Amish. Was Sharon so smitten she was thinking about walking away from her faith? Cheryl believed strongly that people had to find their own way. Levi had left the church, but it wasn't something Cheryl took lightly. She didn't want to see Sharon throw away a lifetime of belief for a man who didn't seem to know she was alive. Sharon's actions were more like those of a teenager, but if she'd lived a very sheltered life, expecting her to act with more maturity was probably unreasonable.

Cheryl saw Levi, Rebecca, and Anton sitting in the middle of the crowded restaurant. She was glad to see they'd gotten a table. Sometimes there could be a long wait at Yoder's. Cheryl waved at them as she and Sharon weaved through the tables toward them. When they sat down, Rebecca giggled and pointed at half a cookie on the tray of her high chair.

"Oh, Levi. You let her have a cookie before lunch?" Cheryl said.

He smiled. "It was either that or she was going to say hello to everyone in the restaurant."

Cheryl couldn't help but laugh.

"I've never met such a friendly child," Anton said. "I think she would have waved at every single person in here if we hadn't found a way to distract her."

"Blame it on me," someone said from behind Cheryl. "I am the one who gave her the cookie."

Charity, one of the regular waitresses from the restaurant, stepped up next to Cheryl.

"Are you sure you're not just trying to keep my husband out of trouble?" Cheryl asked.

"I promise," Charity said, smiling. "It is all my fault."

Cheryl laughed again. "Okay, Levi's out of the doghouse. And between you and me, it was a pretty good idea. Rebecca loves cookies."

"She and I are alike then." Charity looked around the table. "What can I get you all to drink?"

After they gave her their orders, Charity left with a promise to come back and find out what they wanted for lunch.

Cheryl leaned over and kissed Rebecca's cheek. "How are you, Boo Bear?" she asked.

"Mama, Mama, Mama . . ." she replied, holding out a piece of rather masticated cookie.

"No thank you, sweetie," Cheryl said. "But you are very sweet to offer."

Satisfied she'd done all she could, Rebecca stuck most of the piece in her mouth and started chewing.

"I'm glad to see you again, Sharon," Anton said with a smile.

Sharon blushed. "I am happy to see you as well." She cleared her throat. "I have asked Cheryl if I could stay in town a little longer."

"Really?" Anton frowned. "What is there about Sugarcreek that makes you want to hang around here?" The pink spots on Sharon's cheeks darkened. "I do not get out much at home. Being here is a treat for me. I hate to leave." She looked down toward her lap. "I have made such special friends, it is hard to say goodbye."

"You're very sweet," Anton said. "I hope I'm one of the friends you're talking about."

"Ja, of course you are," Sharon said. She raised her head and gave Anton a small smile.

Cheryl caught Levi's eye and raised an eyebrow. He looked a little surprised but controlled it quickly. "So, would you like us to recommend something?" he asked Anton and Sharon.

"I still remember the great food here," Anton said.

Levi shook his head. "Sometimes I forget you lived here. You have been gone so long."

"Well, you might have forgotten, but it seems not everyone else has."

Levi frowned at him. "I do not understand what you mean."

"Look around. If looks could kill..."

Cheryl gazed around the room. Sure enough, they were being checked out by quite a few customers. And most of them didn't look happy. Cheryl noticed several people she knew. She smiled at them but not many returned her smile. Embarrassed, she turned her attention back to her menu even though she knew it by heart. This was what Levi had warned her about, but now that she was experiencing it, she still found it surprising. Sugarcreek was a friendly village, full of warm people. Even during some difficult circumstances in the past, she'd felt support. But if the expressions on some of these faces were representative of the feelings they had toward Anton—and possibly her and Levi—a lot of that support seemed to have vanished.

"I am sorry people judge you without cause," Sharon said. "It is not the Amish way. We believe in love and forgiveness."

"Maybe you do," Anton mumbled, "but I haven't been shown a lot of that."

"We may not be members of the Amish church," Levi said, "but we believe in you."

Cheryl smiled at Anton, glad Levi had said what she'd wanted to. The stares Anton was getting made her angry and even more committed to treating her guest with kindness.

Anton sighed. "To be honest, I don't blame them anymore. Liesel has been missing over ten years. We were close. I met with her many times even though I'd been told not to, and then she disappeared. Maybe if the positions had been reversed I would feel the same way. I might as well accept that the only way I'll ever be really exonerated in the minds of these people is if Liesel shows up. One way or another."

Cheryl knew what he meant, but she still hoped Liesel would be found alive, even though as time passed it looked less and less likely.

Suddenly Cheryl heard a few gasps and turned to see August Yoder striding quickly toward their table. He was a chubby man who loved his own cooking. His round face was void of its usual smile. Instead, he looked determined, as if he were on a mission. And he was headed right toward them.

Cheryl looked at Levi, whose eyes were trained on August. He looked worried. Was August going to ask Anton to leave the restaurant? Cheryl gulped and turned her attention to Anton, who also watched August approach. Anton's expression was a mixture of anger . . . and fear.

CHAPTER TWENTY

Before any of them could say or do anything, August stomped up to the table. "Anton Birken," he said loudly enough for everyone in the restaurant to hear him. He reached out his hand and slowly Anton took it. August shook his hand with gusto. "Greta and I are so sorry about your mother. Please accept our condolences. Even though your trip home is because of sad circumstances, we are both so happy to see you."

From behind him, Greta hurried to stand next to her husband, her equally round face flushed red with exertion. "We have missed you, boy," she said with a smile. She leaned over and gave him a quick hug.

Cheryl was touched to see tears spring to Anton's eyes. "Th-thank you," he choked out.

"Anything you want is on the house," August said. Cheryl had always loved the kind couple, and at that moment, her respect for them also increased. She felt herself getting emotional too.

Anton was trying to say something else but couldn't get the words out. Suddenly, Rebecca held her arms out to Greta. "Hi, hi, hi!" she sang out, causing Greta and several people around them to laugh.

Greta hugged the happy little girl who then pointed at the tray on her high chair and said, "Mo cookie?"

This time almost everyone in the restaurant laughed. Cheryl noticed one dour-looking couple get up and walk out, but all the other customers sent smiles their way.

"You can certainly have another cookie if Mama says it is okay," Greta said, a wide smile splitting her face.

"Maybe after she eats her lunch," Cheryl said. She reached over and grabbed Greta's hand. "Thank you, Greta." The words caught in her throat.

"Ach, liebling, you are more than welcome." She leaned down and gave Cheryl a hug.

"That is enough hugging and crying," August declared, blinking away his own tears. "Now...let us eat! What can I make for you, my friend?" he asked Anton.

"I...I always loved your bologna sandwiches."

"I will make you the best bologna sandwich you have ever eaten," August declared. He waved Charity over to the table. "Take their orders and deliver them to me. I will take special care with each dish." He strode out of the dining room just as dramatically as he'd entered. After he left, Cheryl realized the ambience of the room had changed. The tension was gone, and those sitting at tables around them seemed more relaxed. August had changed the entire tone with his bold act of graciousness.

Charity came over and took their orders. Cheryl selected her favorite meal, chicken and dumplings. The portions at Yoder's were huge, so she asked for a small plate for Rebecca so they could share. There would be enough for both of them with some left over.

Levi ordered chicken-fried steak, and Sharon joined Cheryl by ordering the chicken and dumplings. When Charity brought the coffee Cheryl had ordered, she grabbed it like a drowning person reaching for a lifeline. She was tired. Worrying about Anton, Douglas and Joni, and the recent thefts in Sugarcreek had taken their toll.

The rest of their lunch was very enjoyable. Anton told them some stories of his life in Sugarcreek when he was young. He'd been an adventurous child and some of his antics were funny, although Cheryl wasn't too sure she'd be laughing if Rebecca did some of the things Anton had.

Sharon also shared some of her life in Bird-in-Hand. It sounded a lot like Sugarcreek. Levi knew some of the people who lived there. It was interesting to see how connected the two towns were.

When they finished their lunch, Charity came back to encourage them to order dessert, but everyone was too full. Even though August had told them lunch was on him, Levi asked for the bill. Charity confirmed that their entire meal was on the house. As they were leaving, Cheryl found Greta and thanked her again for her kindness.

"Ach, Cheryl. It is not hard to be kind to those you love. The hard part is being kind to those who are hard to love."

"You certainly seem to understand that better than I do," Cheryl said with a sigh.

"You do not give yourself enough credit," Greta said gently. "I have watched you ever since you came to Sugarcreek. You have loved the unlovely more than once. I am so glad you are a part of this town. We are richer because of it."

Cheryl felt her eyes fill with tears at Greta's kind words. "No, I am the richer one," she said.

"I guess we will have to agree to disagree," Greta said, her eyes wet too.

Levi called out Cheryl's name. He stood by the front door with Rebecca in his arms.

"I'd better get going," Cheryl said to Greta. "Thank you again."

"You're welcome," Greta said. "You have a great day with that lovely family of yours. And if there is anything we can do for Anton, please let us know. He was a rather wild boy, but he always had a good heart. August used to hire him for small jobs when he was a kid. He never let August down. We never believed he hurt Liesel. She was a very unhappy girl who wanted to live a different kind of life. I know her parents do not admit to this, but it is true. I pray she is alive somewhere and living the life she wanted."

"I do too." Cheryl smiled at Greta and then met Levi at the door.

"Are we going to the shop now?" he asked when Cheryl reached him.

"Sure, if Anton wants to see it. I guess the last time he was inside was when Aunt Mitzi owned it."

Levi nodded. "That would be correct."

He opened the front door, and Cheryl stepped outside onto the front porch. "Where are Sharon and Anton?" she asked.

"They decided to walk to the shop," Levi said. Cheryl looked down the street. Sure enough, the couple was walking down the sidewalk in the direction of the shop.

"I thought Amish women weren't supposed to be alone with men...especially men who aren't Amish," Cheryl said frowning.

"So my *Englisch* wife is worried about Amish customs now?"

"Of course not. It's just that...Well, I'm a little concerned about Sharon. I'd like to return her to Bird-in-Hand in the same condition she arrived here."

Levi laughed. "I do not believe you are in charge of Sharon—or Anton. It might be best to let them work out their own lives. Besides, they are not alone. They are out on a public street where everyone can see them. Do not worry."

They walked over to Cheryl's car. Levi put Rebecca in her car seat while Cheryl got behind the wheel. Since they'd both driven to the restaurant, they'd have to drive their own vehicles to the shop.

"I need to spend some time working with Esther," Cheryl said. "Can you take Rebecca for the afternoon?"

"Sure," Levi said. "If it is okay, I might have Maam watch her for a while. Anton and I want to visit some of the places where we used to spend time."

"That's fine. Have you talked to him about how you acted toward him before he left town?"

The smile slipped from Levi's face. "No, but I will soon. I intend to do that today. He does not seem to hold a grudge, but I still feel the need to apologize. I cannot offer an excuse for my actions, but I can certainly ask his forgiveness."

"If it makes any difference, I think he forgave you a long time ago," Cheryl said. "He treats you like a friend. I don't see any resentment in his reaction toward you."

"Ja, I see the same thing." Levi sighed. "And somehow it makes me feel even worse."

"You're a good man, Levi," Cheryl said softly. "He knows that. I do too. Maybe the person you need to forgive is yourself."

Levi finished strapping Rebecca in her car seat. He kissed her forehead and then walked around the car to Cheryl's window. He leaned down and kissed her. "Thank you. You may be right...as usual. I am blessed to have you for my wife. Have I told you that enough?"

Cheryl chuckled. "You tell me that all the time. I feel the same way about you, although I have no idea why."

Levi straightened up. "Well of course you do. I am a very handsome man."

Cheryl snorted. "Very funny. Now go away."

Levi put on a hurt expression. "I feel rather abused."

"You will be if you don't get away from my car."

He laughed and jogged over to his truck. From her car seat, Rebecca giggled. She might not understand her father's humor, but she certainly recognized the joy in his laughter.

Cheryl smiled to herself. At that moment, she felt blessed beyond measure.

Chapter Twenty-One

B y the time Cheryl reached the shop and took Rebecca out of
her car seat, Sharon and Anton had already arrived. When she
got inside, Esther and Joni were showing Anton around.

"Things have definitely changed since I was here," he told
Cheryl with a smile. "You've expanded. And there are a lot more
items." He pointed to the coolers that held cheeses, pies, cakes,
and other pastries. "I left Yoder's full, but looking at all this good
food is making me hungry again."

"Pick something and take it back with you," Cheryl said.

"I was blessed with the same choice," Sharon said. "I hate to
say it, but the chocolate cake I chose is dwindling down quickly in
size."

"I appreciate it," Anton said to Cheryl. "But we might have to
come back later. I don't think we're going by the house for a while."

"You're right," Levi said.

The bell over the front door rang, and Cheryl looked to see
who'd entered. She recognized the teen who stood staring at Joni.
Warren Pope. Joni obviously saw him, but turned away, focusing
her attention on Anton.

"Maybe I could bring dessert to you later," Joni said. "After
work."

Cheryl was surprised at Joni's offer. It was true that they did deliveries from time to time, but since Anton was living on their property, it certainly wasn't necessary.

"That's okay, Joni," she said. "You pick something, Anton. I'll bring it home with me when I leave here."

Anton looked a little unsure but gave her a half-hearted smile. "Thanks, Cheryl. I appreciate the thought, Joni."

"Not a problem." She gave Anton a wide smile. Then she sidled up next to him and took his arm.

"Let me show you our complete selection," she said. "That way you can pick something you'll really enjoy." She led him away, laughing and smiling at him as if they shared a private joke.

Cheryl looked over at Warren. His face was flushed with anger.

"Hi, Warren," Cheryl said. "Is there something I can help you with?"

He scowled at her. "No, thanks," he said abruptly. "I've seen everything I need to see." He turned around and stomped out of the shop.

Cheryl saw Joni glance quickly toward the door, watching Warren leave. Then she turned back to Anton and continued pointing out the various cakes, pies, and other bakery goods in the Swiss Miss's coolers. She let go of Anton's arm and was much more subdued. Although she seemed more like herself, it was clear she'd been flirting with Anton for Warren's benefit. Cheryl had never seen her act like this. She was flabbergasted.

Cheryl felt a hand on her arm. Esther stood next to her. "May I speak to you a moment?" she asked. "In the office?"

"Sure. I'll be right back," she said to Sharon, who was watching Joni and Anton closely. She nodded absentmindedly.

Cheryl followed Esther into the office, and Esther closed the door behind them. "Warren broke up with Joni earlier today. He was angry about Douglas. He thinks Joni should do more to stop the attention he shows her."

"What would he like her to do?" Cheryl asked. "We contacted the police."

"I do not know, but I think she rather enjoyed Warren's jealousy and was not as clear with him as she should have been."

"You mean she didn't make sure Warren knew she wasn't interested in Douglas?"

Esther nodded. "I think this might be true."

"And so she was flirting with Anton to make Warren jealous?"

Esther sighed. "Ja. Perhaps she thinks that seeing her with Anton will cause Warren to fight to win her back."

Cheryl sat on the edge of her desk. "So let's think this through. Warren breaks up with her because he thinks Joni might like Douglas. So her next move is to make him think she likes Anton? Won't that just make Warren more upset?"

Esther shrugged. "I am confused also, but I believe this is her plan."

"She realizes Anton is too old for her, right? Does she know what some people in this town think of him?"

Esther raised her hands and let them fall. "I do not believe she is thinking about these things...or anything. She is just reacting out of hurt. She really does care for Warren. And I believe he cares for her." She sighed. "I am glad Henry and I do not act like this. Being dishonest is always a bad decision. I can see now that it is also very confusing."

Henry Detweiler was a sweet young man who adored Esther. They were getting closer and closer. Cheryl loved Esther like a sister and was happy to see her with someone like Henry.

"Okay." Cheryl thought for a moment. "I'm going to talk to her. Tell her she's not to bother Anton anymore. I told her I'd talk to Douglas, and I will."

"But if the chief has spoken to him..."

"But I want to make it clear I don't want him coming here. The truth is, he has the right to be here since it's a public place. I think a word from me as the owner of the business will help." She frowned at Esther. "Did she speak to her parents? What do they say?"

Esther shook her head. "No, I do not believe she has told them."

Cheryl stood up. "All right. This has to stop. Will you go out there and ask Joni to come into the office? I'm going to give her a chance to speak to her parents—or I'll do it for her. They should know what's going on."

"Thank you, Cheryl," Esther said. "I must admit I am concerned about this." She looked away for a moment. "I do not want to harshly judge anyone without cause, but Douglas Powell makes me uncomfortable. Even after Chief Twitchell spoke to him, he drove by here. I have seen him. And last night he was parked down the street when we closed."

"Well, that settles it," Cheryl said. "I'll speak to him today. I wonder if he's working tonight?"

"I believe he is. Last night he was off." Esther blushed. "I do not like to go to the store when he is there. That is why I know his schedule."

"Okay. Do you know what time his shift starts?"

"Around five o'clock on Thursdays. It is the only evening he works."

"I'll speak to him." Cheryl squeezed Esther's shoulder. "Don't worry, okay?"

Esther smiled, but Cheryl could see the tension in her face. She really was concerned. She left the office, and Cheryl took a seat behind her desk. As she waited, she tried to figure out what to say to Joni. A few minutes later, the door opened and Joni walked in, her expression guarded.

"Esther said you wanted to see me," she said.

Cheryl pointed at the chairs in front of her desk. "Yes, I do. Sit down, please."

Joni's pouty expression emphasized her youth. Cheryl felt a tug of compassion for her, but at the same time, she recognized how important it was that Joni understand the possible consequences of her actions.

"I want you to know how much I appreciate your hard work here," Cheryl said. "You're a good worker, and I'm glad we hired you."

"Are...are you firing me?" Joni's eyes widened with fear.

"No, Joni," Cheryl said quickly. "That's not why I called you in here." She frowned at the young girl. "I'm afraid for you. Some of the choices you're making are...ill-advised."

"What do you mean?"

"Well, for example, the way you're acting toward Anton Birken."

"You think he's really guilty of hurting that girl?"

Cheryl sighed. This wasn't going the way she'd intended. "No, I don't. That's not my point. I'm trying to tell you that someone your age shouldn't be...showing that much attention to a man Anton's age. Trying to make your boyfriend jealous isn't a good reason to act inappropriately."

Joni's eyebrows shot up. "Esther told you what I said about Warren." She shook her head. "That's the last time I trust her with anything."

"Joni, she's worried about you. The way a real friend should be. I'm concerned too."

"I told you it would be okay. Besides, it's my business."

"Not when you flirt with a friend of mine—in my store. That makes it my business." Cheryl didn't like the harshness in her response, but she wasn't sure how to get through to the girl. "Look," she said slowly, trying to rein in her temper. "Here's the thing. I'm going to talk to Douglas myself. Tell him I don't want him hanging around the Swiss Miss." She crossed her arms over her chest. "Did you tell your parents about Douglas?"

"Sure. They're not worried."

"You didn't tell them, did you?"

Joni's silence told Cheryl what she needed to know. "They have to know, Joni. You're their child. Parents need to be aware of situations like this."

Joni didn't respond. "I want you to tell your parents what's going on. Immediately. If you don't, I'll have to."

Joni's sharp intake of breath made it clear that Cheryl had hit a nerve. "Please don't tell them. They might not let me see Warren anymore."

Cheryl frowned at her. "What does this have to do with Warren? Besides, I thought you already broke up."

Joni shifted uncomfortably in her chair. "My parents think I'm too young to date. It took a lot of talking to get them to let me go to the movies with Warren. Now all this is happening. If they find out about it, they'll decide it was all a big mistake." She shook her head. "Warren broke up with me, but I know he still likes me. I can get him back." She scowled at Cheryl. "As long as things don't get weird."

"By weird, you mean if your parents interfere in some way?"

"Yeah. If I tell them about Douglas, they'll freak out. Decide I shouldn't be dating at all. I don't want to lose Warren because Douglas won't leave me alone." She gave Cheryl a look of disgust. "Do you know they even threatened to call Warren's parents before we went to the movies? Get to know them better? Have you ever heard of anything so awful? Warren would think I'm a baby!"

Cheryl had to bite her lip to keep from laughing. She took a deep breath. "Look, no matter what, you need to talk to your parents."

"They'll ground me forever, and I'll never see Warren again." The girl's lower lip trembled.

"They won't ground you forever. I want you to go home, Joni. Don't come back to work until you've spoken to your parents. And

I will check." Cheryl stood up. "I'm not trying to be mean. I really just want you to make things right. For your own benefit. Do you understand?"

Joni stood slowly to her feet. "I think I do. I'll tell them tonight at supper." She wiped away a single tear that fell down her cheek. "Do I really have to leave? Can't I stay until closing? My parents are at work. I can't talk to them until tonight anyway."

Cheryl considered her request. Although she understood Joni's point, she felt strongly she should hold her ground. "No, you go on home. It will give you time to think about what to say to your folks. We'll see you tomorrow, Joni."

"Okay." She stood up. "I really like working here, Cheryl. I don't want to lose my job."

"I value you and your work. Just make things right with your mom and dad and then come back."

Joni nodded. "Thank you. I'm sorry this got so goofed up. You're a great boss, and Esther is a good friend. I don't want to mess up my relationship with either one of you."

Cheryl walked around the table and put her arms around the young girl. Thankfully, Joni hugged her back. When Cheryl released her, she smiled at the upset teenager. "Everything will be okay. I'm going to talk to Douglas today. If I don't get the response I want, I'll talk to the chief again. I have a feeling Douglas's days of bothering you are coming to an end. I can't help you with Warren, but I hope you can straighten things out with him."

"I hope so. Maybe Warren will talk to me again if Douglas will leave me alone."

Cheryl shook her head. "Maybe, but let's concentrate on straightening everything out with your parents first."

Joni turned and walked toward the door. Before walking out, she turned back to look at Cheryl. "I know you're trying to help me, Cheryl. Thanks."

"You're welcome. I really do care about you, Joni."

"I know that."

As Joni closed the door behind her, Cheryl prayed that they were on the way to putting all this drama behind them. Not only for her sake, but for Joni's as well.

Chapter Twenty-Two

When Cheryl came back into the shop, she found Anton and Sharon talking quietly near the front door. Esther was helping a customer, and Levi had taken Rebecca outside. They were sitting on a bench on the front porch of the shop.

"I am going to walk back to the cottage," Sharon said when she saw Cheryl.

"I can drive you," Cheryl said.

Sharon shook her head. "The cottage is not far. I would like to walk."

When Cheryl lived at the cottage, she'd walked to work many times. She smiled at Sharon. "I'll pick you up a little after five for supper."

"That sounds lovely. I need to rest a bit. I am not used to all this activity."

"I guess I'll see you tonight," Anton said with a smile.

It didn't take much guesswork to see that Sharon was attracted to Anton. Cheryl wondered if Levi saw it too.

"I'm going to talk to Levi for a moment," she said. "I'll be right back."

Sharon nodded but stayed where she was, next to Anton. Cheryl stepped around them and went outside where Levi smiled at her.

"I think we will be going," he said. "When will you be home?"

"I'll probably stay until closing since Joni isn't here. I think we're in pretty good shape for the festival, but I want to double-check everything one more time. After today, I should be home more. Until the festival, of course."

"Maam will be glad to help you," Levi said. "I will probably be needed to assist with the petting zoo and the corn maze."

Cheryl smiled at him. "We'll work it out. We always do."

Levi cocked his head toward the door. "Is Anton ready to go?"

Cheryl sat down next to him on the bench and lowered her voice. "He's talking to Sharon. Have you noticed they seem to be getting closer?"

Levi shrugged. "She is Amish, and he was raised Amish. I believe they are talking about their similarities. Sharon could be a big help to him, I think. She seems to have a calming effect."

"I hope you're right." Cheryl sighed. "I sent Joni home. The way she acted around Anton..."

"It embarrassed him."

"I'm not surprised. She hasn't told her parents about Douglas."

Levi frowned. "They need to know."

"She promised she would tell them tonight at supper. I'm going by the grocery store on the way home and speak to Douglas."

Levi's eyebrows shot up. "You certainly are not."

"Excuse me?"

"I do not want you to confront him, Cheryl. I mean it."

Cheryl shook her head. "I promised…"

"I do not care."

Rebecca, who had been content to watch the people walking down the street, suddenly reached out for her mother. Cheryl took her. "Levi, I need to tell Douglas to stay away from the shop. I'll be talking to him at the grocery store. Surrounded by people."

"No, you will not. You will come home and watch Rebecca. I will speak to Douglas."

Cheryl considered his offer. "But you don't work at the Swiss Miss."

Levi laughed. "No, but I am married to the owner. And I am a man. In this situation, I believe you need a man to issue a warning."

Cheryl grinned. "Do you think he'll be afraid of an Amish man?"

"But I have left the Amish church. I am an ex-Amish man who will not allow people to mess with his wife or her employees. Who knows what I am capable off?"

Cheryl laughed heartily. "Well, when you put it that way…"

Levi leaned over and kissed Cheryl on the cheek. "I am not trying to order you around, Cheryl, but I do not want you to put yourself in danger. Let me talk to Douglas. Even though you think I am not scary, I believe I can fool Douglas Powell."

"Okay, if it's that important to you. But you tell him I said he's not welcome in my store anymore, okay?"

"I will issue your warning."

"Thanks. Are you planning to take Rebecca with you on your tour of the past?"

Levi nodded. "It will not take us long. Sugarcreek is not very big. We do not have that many places to visit."

Cheryl smiled at him. "Okay." She glanced at her watch. "I'll leave a little early. That way you can issue Douglas your warning and get back in time for supper."

"That sounds good. Will you tell Anton we need to leave?"

"Yeah, but let me say goodbye to my Boo Bear first." Cheryl hugged her daughter and then handed her to Levi. Rebecca started to blubber and cry out, "Mama, Mama, Mama..." Obviously, she was missing her mother. Cheryl would be glad when she had more time at home and wasn't needed as much at the store. She loved the Swiss Miss, but she loved being a mother more.

She waved at Levi and Rebecca as he carried her to the truck. Cheryl had no idea what he said to their daughter, but by the time he put her in her car seat, she was laughing.

Cheryl went back into the store. Sharon almost looked surprised to see her.

"Levi is getting ready to leave," she told Anton.

"Okay." He smiled at Sharon. "I'll see you tonight at dinner."

Sharon smiled back at him. "Yes, I will see you then."

Anton said goodbye to Cheryl and hurried out to the truck. Once he climbed inside, Levi drove away.

"Oh, my," Sharon said. "The time just slipped away from me." She smiled at Cheryl. "I will be going as well. I will be ready to leave at five."

She said goodbye and set off for the cottage. Esther came up to Cheryl after checking out a customer's purchases.

"May I ask why Joni left early?" she said.

"Of course," Cheryl said. She briefly explained her conversation with Joni and her reasons for sending her home. As she talked, Esther kept nodding. Hopefully, it was because she agreed with Cheryl's actions. Turned out she had no reason to worry.

"I think that was wise," she said when Cheryl finished. "I do not like Joni keeping secrets from her parents. I've learned the hard way that is always a mistake."

"I agree," Cheryl said. "I'm hoping that after tonight, our problem will be solved. With Joni talking to her parents and Levi speaking to Douglas, I think our bases should be covered."

"Except for Warren," Esther said quietly, almost as an afterthought.

"Let's let Joni's parents deal with that situation," Cheryl said. "I'm through parenting children who don't even belong to me."

Esther giggled. "I believe that is a good decision."

As Cheryl and Esther got to work, Cheryl began to wonder if Levi's visit with Douglas would help—or cause more problems than they already had.

CHAPTER TWENTY-THREE

Cheryl left the store around 3:30. She wanted to get home so Levi could go talk to Douglas without having to take Rebecca with him.

She was almost out of town when she noticed a woman walking down the street, not far from Buttons 'n Bows, Gail Murray's shop. As she looked closer, she recognized the woman who'd stolen Sharon's quilt. Cheryl quickly pulled over. She ran into Gail's shop. Gail was talking to a customer, but Cheryl interrupted her.

"Gail, the gal who stole from us is walking down the sidewalk. Will you please call the police? If they can get here in time, maybe we can catch her."

Gail excused herself from talking to her customer. She ran over and grabbed her purse from under the counter, pulled out her phone, and started dialing.

"You go on," she told Cheryl. "I'll get the police here. Which way was she going?"

Cheryl told her and then ran out the door. As she ran after the woman, several people she knew tried to stop her and talk, but she told them she couldn't speak to them.

It took two full blocks before she spotted the woman again. She pulled back a bit and slowed down. She didn't want the woman to see her. In a footrace, Cheryl was pretty sure the younger woman could beat her. The only chance she had to catch her was to keep her from becoming suspicious.

The woman crossed the third block but then suddenly seemed to disappear. Cheryl increased her speed and hurried to where she'd lost track of her. She found herself standing in front of a vacant building. It had belonged to an insurance agency that closed when the owner retired. Could she be inside? Cheryl went up to the front door and tried to open it. Locked.

When her phone rang, she almost jumped out of her skin. She quickly answered it.

"Cheryl, it's Gail. The chief is here. Where are you?"

Cheryl told her about losing the girl near the vacant building. "I'm wondering if she's inside, Gail. Maybe she's been staying here. It would explain the things she's taken. Blankets, our quilt, food, clothes... I'm thinking she might be homeless."

"Well, I'm sorry about that, but I'd rather donate things from my store, not have them stolen."

"I agree. Tell the chief to get here right away. I'll watch the building."

"I will. Don't lose her!"

"I'll do my best."

Gail disconnected, and Cheryl put her phone in her pocket. She decided to check around the back of the building. As she rounded the side, she looked at the windows. They all seemed to be intact. But when she found the back door, she saw immediately that it had been forced. She started to pull on it when the door suddenly flew open. The woman she'd been following stood in front of her. But as Cheryl looked at her face, she realized this wasn't a woman at all. Their thief was a girl. Maybe fifteen or sixteen. Cheryl was so surprised, she just stood there. Before she could say anything, the girl took off. She was so fast, there wasn't any way Cheryl could catch her. The girl cut between two other buildings and disappeared.

A few minutes later, she heard the chief's voice calling her name. She hurried around the building until she saw him standing by the front door.

"That door is locked, Chief," she called out. "The door in the back isn't."

The chief walked toward her. "I want you to get back," he said gruffly. "Stand on the sidewalk and tell my officers where I am when they get here."

"Not necessary," Cheryl said. "Our thief just ran away."

"Which way did she go?"

Cheryl pointed out the girl's path but told the chief, "She's long gone. And Chief, it's not a woman. She's a teenager. A girl."

The chief shook his head. "I'm going in. You stay here. Just in case she has partners helping her out."

She would have liked to go inside with Chief Twitchell, but she recognized the chief was trying to protect her.

The chief disappeared. A couple of minutes later two patrol cars pulled in front of the abandoned insurance agency. Two officers jumped out and ran up to Cheryl. She recognized Officers Ortega and Spencer.

"Where is he?" Officer Ortega asked.

Cheryl pointed toward the rear of the building. "The back door is unlocked. He's inside."

"Is our subject inside as well?" Officer Spencer asked.

"No, she's gone. The chief's making sure she was alone."

Officer Ortega nodded. "You stay here. We'll check..."

Her next words faded as the chief came around the side of the building. He waved at them. "Back here," he called out. "You might as well come along, Cheryl."

Surprised to be included, Cheryl followed the officers to where the chief waited.

"You're right. She's gone," he said as Cheryl approached. "I doubt she'll be back." He gestured toward the broken door. "You need to see this."

Cheryl followed the chief into the darkened building. Obviously, the electricity had been turned off. The building was chilly, even colder than it was outside, probably because the windows had been covered with cardboard, which kept out any sunshine.

The chief gestured toward a room that must have been an office when the business was open. He shone a flashlight around. A rickety table was covered with food wrappers. Trash overflowed from a battered trash can. The chief swung the flashlight toward the floor, and Cheryl gasped.

"Sharon's quilt!" she said.

Next to the quilt was a pillow.

"This girl's been livin' here," the chief said.

Cheryl felt a twinge of guilt. But why should she feel responsible? The girl was a thief. She sighed loudly. "She's probably a runaway," she said. "And now she's gone."

The chief shrugged. "Not your fault. Don't even go there. The girl made the decision to steal. I'll check the database for runaways. Maybe I can find her."

"Thanks, Chief." Cheryl understood the chief's point of view, but she still felt bad. The girl wasn't a hardened criminal. Just a young, scared kid. Everything she took was something she needed to survive.

"We'll go over the whole place," the chief said, "but it'll take a while. I doubt we'll find anything that will tell us where she went. You might as well go on."

"What about the quilt?" Cheryl asked. "I'd like to get it back."

"I'll make a note of that," said the chief. "Right now it's evidence, but as soon as I can I'll make sure it gets back to you."

Cheryl thanked him and went outside. She scanned the area from the back of the empty building and from the front, but she didn't see the girl anywhere. She walked back to her car where Gail was waiting for her.

"Did you catch her?" Gail asked.

Cheryl shook her head. "She got away. She was living in those old insurance offices. I saw some of your things there. Not everything though. I got a closer look at her, Gail. She's just a kid."

The look on Gail's face mirrored Cheryl's emotions. "Homeless?"

"Seems like it. I'm guessing she's a runaway."

Gail frowned. "Who would escape to Sugarcreek? I mean, aren't there more exciting places to go if you're running away from home?"

"You know, you're right," Cheryl said. "I hadn't really thought of it. That does seem odd. I suppose she could be on her way to somewhere else."

"Maybe." Gail crossed her arms over her chest. "You know, I should be angry because of the things she stole from me, but right now I feel awful. Any idea where she went?"

"Not a clue. Maybe we'll see her again. If we can get her to talk to us, perhaps we can help her."

"Thanks, Cheryl," Gail said. "I'd like that. I'd better get back to work. Will you let me know if you hear anything about her?"

"I certainly will," Cheryl said.

Gail turned around and went back inside her shop.

Cheryl got into her car and drove toward her house, but she couldn't get the young girl out of her mind.

Chapter Twenty-Four

B y the time she got home, Cheryl's thoughts had shifted to Levi's visit with Douglas. What was he going to say? How would Douglas react? Levi certainly wasn't a fighter. What if Douglas attacked him? Of course, being at the store where he worked should make him think twice about that. She hoped so anyway.

Levi was waiting for her when she walked in the door.

"I thought you planned to be here earlier," he said.

"I did. Something happened." She looked around. "Where's Rebecca?"

"She was really tired after hanging around with me and Anton. She's sleeping."

Cheryl sat down and told him about trying to catch the girl and finding out she'd been living in the empty insurance building.

"I am not sure you should have chased her," he said, his expression serious. "What if she had been violent? Had a weapon?"

"She's just a girl, Levi."

"This is the same girl who has been stealing things all over town?"

Cheryl sighed. "I know. It's just...I don't know. Maybe it's because I'm a mother. I would never want Rebecca to feel so lost she had to run away from us. This girl probably has parents who are looking for her."

"The chief should be looking for missing teenagers."

"Yeah, he said he would. I hope he can find out who she is. And then find her. Oh, Levi. Where could she have gone? It's supposed to rain tonight. What if she's out in the elements?"

Levi wrapped his arms around his wife. "You have a soft heart, my love. We will pray for the girl, ja? Pray for her protection and pray that she will find her way home."

"As long as home is a good place," Cheryl said. "Are we doing everything we can to give Rebecca a good home? We have to be great parents, Levi. Really great parents."

Levi pulled back and gazed into Cheryl's eyes. "We are great parents, Cheryl. God knows this because He gave us a wonderful child." He smiled and brushed a strand of hair back from her forehead. "Any child would be blessed to have you for a mother. You must trust God and simply be the incredible woman you are. With God's help, Rebecca will be fine."

"I pray you're right."

"I am." Levi kissed her forehead. "Now, I must go. I need to get to the grocery store before Douglas leaves for the day. I am not sure of his schedule."

Cheryl put her purse on a nearby chair. "Esther said he starts at five so you should be fine. What are you going to say to him, Levi? I'm a little concerned about this."

Levi sighed. "I am going to tell him that his attention to Joni is misplaced due to his age. He is making Joni uncomfortable. We are requesting that he stay away from her—and from our shop when she is working. If he will not do this, I will speak to his boss at the grocery store."

Cheryl snorted. "Seriously?"

Levi shrugged. "Chief Twitchell says there is not much he can do at this point. I think Douglas's employer might be interested in the way his employee acts when he is not at work."

Cheryl grinned at her husband. "You're pretty clever, you know that?"

Levi shrugged and donned an innocent look. "I assumed you already knew this."

Laughing, Cheryl shooed him out of the house. "Supper will be at six."

As Levi got into his truck and drove away, Cheryl thought about how much easier it would be if he could pick up Sharon and bring her to the house for supper. But she wouldn't get in a car with a man unless there was another woman present. Another argument for putting Sharon in the dawdy haus and Anton in the cottage. As soon as Anton left, Cheryl was determined that the roof would be fixed so this kind of situation wouldn't happen again.

She heard Rebecca fussing in the other room and went in. After changing her, she brought her into the kitchen and put her in her high chair. She gave her a juice box and some animal crackers, then bustled around the kitchen, pulling out some ground beef, a jar of spaghetti sauce, and a package of spaghetti. With an Italian salad and some garlic bread, it would all make a nice meal for supper. She prepared the spaghetti, added some oregano and garlic powder, then dumped it in her Crock-Pot and put it on warm.

Levi got back just as Rebecca was ready to get down from her high chair.

"Give me the quick version," she said as she grabbed her jacket and her purse.

Levi frowned. "Douglas has agreed to leave Joni alone but…"

"But what? Did something happen?"

Levi shook his head. "No. He said all the right things, it is just…I am not sure I believed him. He makes me feel… uncomfortable."

"Yeah, me too," Cheryl said. She kissed him quickly. "I've got to pick up Sharon. Would you take care of Rebecca? She just had a juice box and some animal crackers." She frowned at Levi. "Where is Anton?"

"He is in the dawdy haus. He wanted some time to himself before supper. I took him with me to the store, but I asked him to wait in the truck while I talked to Douglas. I did not feel it was appropriate to bring him into the situation. I wanted Douglas to feel as if our conversation was just between us."

"That sounds wise." Cheryl gestured toward the Crock-Pot. "The spaghetti is done. I'll make the salad and the bread when I get home. We have some cake left for dessert."

"I will make the salad and set the table," Levi said.

"You are an excellent husband," Cheryl said with a smile. "Have I ever told you that?"

"Frequently. Especially when I help you."

Cheryl giggled. Rebecca, who was tired of being in her high chair, began to wail.

"I will take care of her," Levi said. "See you soon."

Cheryl rushed out of the house and to her car. It took her about fifteen minutes to reach the cottage. As usual, Sharon was watching for her and came out immediately.

"I am sorry you must come after me every day," she said as she got into the car.

"Not a problem," Cheryl said. "I'm just glad you're here. Have you changed your bus schedule yet?"

Sharon's face flushed pink, and she looked away. "Not yet. I...I am not certain when I want to leave."

"Okay," Cheryl said. "Of course you're welcome to stay as long as you want, but won't your mother be missing you?"

"Cheryl, you have been so gracious to me. I do not wish to be deceitful with you."

"Deceitful? What do you mean?" Even as she asked the question, she thought she knew the answer. The personal conversations with Anton, the walk she took with him...

"Anton and I have a lot in common," Sharon said slowly. "As we talk about our experiences in the Amish life, we have found..." She cleared her throat.

"You've developed feelings for each other?" Cheryl asked.

"Ja, we have." She turned to look at Cheryl. "This was not planned. I have always been happy with my life except..."

"Except?"

"Sometimes I feel as if I would like to know more about a world I am ignorant of. Not the bad things. I do not mean..."

"You don't need to explain it to me," Cheryl said with a smile. "Levi went through all the same feelings."

"You have found happiness together," Sharon said. "Maybe the same will be true for Anton and me."

Cheryl searched for words that wouldn't discourage Sharon, but she was concerned about this turn of events. "Sharon, Levi and I knew each other for years before we made the decision to be together. You've only known Anton a couple of days. That's not long enough to decide anything."

"You think I am naive because I do not have much experience with men."

"Frankly, yes. Has Anton actually asked you to stay? Has he told you he's interested in a relationship?"

Sharon blushed again. "No, he has not. But I am certain he feels the same way I do."

Cheryl felt her heart sink. It was true that Anton seemed interested in Sharon, but what if his attention wasn't based on anything serious? The young woman had lived a very sheltered life and didn't know the difference between flirting and real romantic feelings.

"Sharon, I hope you will guard your heart. It's possible Anton doesn't feel the same way you do. I...I don't want to see you get hurt."

"I understand, Cheryl. I will be careful."

Even though she said the right thing, Cheryl felt strongly Sharon didn't mean it. She didn't talk much the rest of the way home.

Cheryl was troubled. Concern about the runaway girl, Joni, and now Sharon weighed heavily on her heart.

CHAPTER TWENTY-FIVE

Although dinner was pleasant, Sharon was unusually quiet. Levi gave Cheryl a questioning look, but she couldn't get a chance to talk to him privately. It would have to wait until after she took Sharon home.

"The funeral service starts at ten o'clock," Cheryl said to Sharon. "Do you still want to watch Rebecca?"

"Ja, I am happy to do so," she said.

"I'll bring her by around nine, if it's okay. I want to pick up some rolls, and we need time to get there." She looked at Anton. "I assume you want to arrive a little early."

"I'm not sure," he said. "Since I doubt I'll be welcome, maybe it's best to show up right before the sermon starts so people will have something to focus on rather than me."

"I hope it will not be too uncomfortable," Levi said. "You have not spoken to your sister?"

Anton shook his head. "I haven't tried to reach out to her. I think it would be a waste of time."

"But she is not angry with you because of the missing girl?" Sharon said. "She is upset because you left?"

Anton nodded. "I don't think she believes I had anything to do with Liesel's disappearance. Anyway, I hope she doesn't. She thinks my leaving hurt my mother. Caused her death."

164 | Sugarcreek Amish Mysteries

"Ten years later?" Levi said. "That does not make sense to me."

"Or to me," Anton said. "Trying to reason with Meredith is a lost cause. She's just angry. At me."

Sharon cleared her throat. "Maybe she is really angry that you left because she misses you, Anton."

"Well, if that's the case, why doesn't she tell me that?" The frustration in his voice was clear. "I really thought I was doing the family a favor. It was terrible back then. When I walked down the street, people whispered about me. People who really knew me..." He suddenly stopped talking and swung his gaze to Levi. "I...I don't mean you, Levi."

Levi put his fork down slowly and met Anton's eyes. "You should," he said in a low voice. "I let you down. I was a terrible friend."

Anton shook his head. "No you weren't. Everyone was concerned about Liesel. And they should have been."

"You're letting me off too easily. I should have stood up for you. I was afraid." Levi's eyes were shiny with tears. "I have regretted it for years. I hope you can forgive me."

Anton, who seemed moved by Levi's words, smiled at him. "I can't forgive you because I was never angry with you. Nor am I now. The sentiment in Sugarcreek back then was strong and pervasive. I wouldn't have allowed you to go to war for me. Life would have been very difficult for you, and I knew I was leaving. There was no reason for it, truly. I always knew you were my friend. When I contacted the chief about finding a place to stay and he told me that you had married and left the church, I asked him to talk to you. I was certain you'd allow me to stay with you."

"I am glad you did," Levi said.

"It's time to let go of guilt, Levi," Anton said.

"Thank you, my friend. I feel as if a great weight has lifted from my shoulders."

"One that you put there yourself," Anton said with a smile.

"Okay, you two," Cheryl said, grinning. "Time to move on."

Anton laughed. "You're right, Cheryl. I wonder if I could get another slice of that delicious garlic bread?"

"Of course." Cheryl got up and went to the oven where she was keeping the bread warm. She took it out and cut off a piece for Anton. "Anyone else?" she asked.

"I would like another slice," Levi said.

Cheryl got two pieces and brought them back to the table.

"This is delicious, Cheryl," Anton said. "I appreciate your cooking for me. I don't think I want to stay for the funeral meal tomorrow. Instead, I'd like to take you all out for lunch. Maybe we could go to the Honey Bee?"

"Thank you, Anton," Cheryl said. "That sounds great."

"We'll come back and get you and Rebecca, Sharon," Anton said.

"That is not necessary," she said. "You three go ahead."

Cheryl watched Anton closely. His face fell. "Please come, Sharon. I'll be leaving on Saturday. I'd like to spend more time with you before then."

Was there something more than just friendship in Anton's request? Suddenly, Cheryl wasn't sure. She glanced at Levi and saw something in his expression that told her he saw the same thing.

"All right," Sharon said. "If it is important to you."

"It is." Anton smiled at her warmly.

Suddenly, he burst out laughing. He was looking at Rebecca, who had decided to adorn her hair in spaghetti. It was so comical everyone laughed, breaking the slight tension.

After cleaning Rebecca up, Cheryl served cake. Then they all decided to make it an early night since they had to prepare for the service the next day.

On the way back to the cottage, Cheryl struggled to find something to say to Sharon that wouldn't upset her.

"Sharon," she said finally, "I'm sorry if I hurt your feelings earlier. It wasn't my intention. I was just concerned that you might confuse Anton's actions for something else. I could be wrong though. Tonight... Well, maybe he does have feelings for you. I think you need to find out."

"I don't know, Cheryl," Sharon said. "I am not offended. I am not sure Anton and I have a future." She sighed. "I have questions about my life. I am not saying I plan to leave the Amish church, but I am curious about the world. In people like you who have faith but express it in a different way. Anton understands my feelings." She smiled at Cheryl. "You might be surprised to learn that Anton wonders from time to time if he might want to rejoin the church. Our bond is one of friendship. There may be something else there, but neither one of us has plans to act on it.

We barely know each other. Right now, we are just trying to find our way through questions of faith. Do you understand?"

Cheryl smiled at her. "Trust me, I understand completely. I was just worried that you two might be getting into something you're not ready for. It seems I had nothing to worry about."

"For now, we are happy to talk and to support each other," Sharon said. "But thank you for your concern. And for your friendship."

After dropping Sharon off, Cheryl began the drive toward home. It was a chilly night. Temperatures had dropped, and the forecast called for rain again. Although Cheryl loved to fall asleep listening to the rain, at that moment, all she could think about was the runaway girl. Where was she? Was she all right? Where was she staying? Was she outside? Cheryl was pretty sure she would have a tough time falling asleep tonight.

By the time she made it home, Levi had already given Rebecca a bath and had her ready for bed. Cheryl spent some time rocking her to sleep and then transferred her to her crib. Levi, who had been cleaning up the kitchen, came into the living room when Cheryl came back from Rebecca's room. Cheryl plopped down on the couch with a sigh. It had been a busy day. Chasing after that girl had exhausted her.

"Maybe a cup of hot chocolate will make you feel better," Levi said, carrying a steaming cup of cocoa. He handed it to Cheryl.

"Oh, thank you," she said with a grateful smile. "Exactly what I need after the kind of day I've had."

Levi sat down next to her. "So what is going on between Sharon and Anton?" he asked. "I believe I saw some sparks there."

Cheryl sighed. "Sharon and Anton have similar backgrounds. Their bond is primarily because of their questions about faith. I think they're noticing some feelings for each other but nothing they plan to do anything about at this point." She shrugged. "We just need to let them work this out. If anything else comes of it...they'll deal with it responsibly, I think. I'm not really worried about them. Besides, it will take a long time before they know for sure that they might have a future together."

Levi shrugged. "Maybe this is a good time for someone to listen to Anton and show him that they care about him."

"I think you're right. Of course, he has you too. You're a good friend, Levi. I hope you feel better now after talking to Anton about the past. He was very gracious. I believe he was being completely honest with you."

"I do feel better. Much better." He sighed. "Now I will do whatever I can to help him through the service tomorrow." Levi exhaled slowly. "I am afraid it will not be easy." He took Cheryl's hand. "You do not have to come with us, you know. It would be perfectly fine for you to stay home with Rebecca."

Cheryl pulled his fingers up to her lips and lightly kissed them. "'Wither thou goest...'"

Levi pulled her close to him. "I don't think that verse is about going to funerals with someone suspected of kidnapping and...worse."

"I think that verse pretty well includes everything," Cheryl whispered. "I'll be by your side, Levi. Always."

He smiled at her and brushed back her bangs. Then he kissed her forehead. "I am so blessed."

"We both are, Levi. We both are."

"You know, I think you are wrong about a couple needing a long time to know they are in love. I fell in love with you the first time I saw you."

"You did not. You barely paid attention to me."

He smiled at her. "You are wrong, Cheryl. You had my heart from the start. It just took time for me to admit how I felt."

As Cheryl thought back, she remembered her reaction when she first met Levi. She was instantly attracted to him, and that attraction only grew the more time they spent around each other. "It's as if we both knew from the beginning," she said softly.

"Ja, and that may be how it is for Sharon and Anton. Time will tell."

A little while later, Levi headed to bed. Cheryl went into the kitchen to put oatmeal in the Crock-Pot for breakfast. She added some butter, some brown sugar, and a little cinnamon. As she set the pot on low, she looked out the kitchen window. Anton was walking out of the dawdy haus. He climbed into his car, started the engine, and backed out of the driveway slowly, without lights. Although he was a grown man and didn't owe them an account of his actions, she found it odd he'd never mentioned his late-night excursions.

She cleaned up the kitchen and headed to bed, troubled by what she'd seen. When she climbed into bed, she found Levi already asleep, Beau snuggled up at his feet. She decided to tell him what she'd seen in the morning. Tomorrow could be a tough day, but before she went to sleep she prayed that God would use the situation to bring healing. Levi had been delivered from leftover guilt today. It would be wonderful to see Anton and his sister find a path back to each other through this difficult time.

As she lay in bed, it started to rain. All she could think about was the homeless girl. As she'd suspected, it took her quite a while to fall asleep.

The next morning, Cheryl hurried around, trying to get ready for the service. She was wearing a plain dress without any kind of adornment. She also covered her hair with a scarf. She was packing toys to take to the cottage so Rebecca would have something to play with while Sharon watched her, when the front doorbell rang. Who in the world would visit this early?

"Can you get the door?" she called out to Levi.

He assured her he was on the way, and Cheryl finished loading up the tote bag and carried it into the living room. Levi was standing near the door. Chief Twitchell and Officer Spencer were with him.

"Is everything okay?" she asked when she saw them.

"No, as a matter of fact it's not," the chief said, his expression tight. "Joni Blanchard has gone missing."

Chapter Twenty-Six

At first, Cheryl couldn't comprehend what the chief had said. It didn't make any sense. Finally, she grasped his meaning. She felt as if she'd been punched in the chest. She gasped for breath, trying to control her emotions.

"What do you mean she's *gone missing*?" she choked out.

"I mean what I said. Her parents called us first thing this mornin'. Her mother went into her room to wake her up, and she was gone. No sign of her. No idea where she might have gone. As you can imagine, they're very upset."

"Maybe she ran away," Levi said. "She didn't want to tell them about Douglas Powell."

The chief shook his head. "No, she told them. When everyone went to bed last night, they were okay. Things had been handled. In fact, Joni's parents, Jerome and AnnMarie, said Joni apologized for not telling them sooner. They were gettin' along better than they had for a while. There wasn't any reason for Joni to take off."

The thought ran through Cheryl's mind that perhaps the parents of the young runaway she'd tracked yesterday thought the same thing before their daughter left home.

"I assume you've been looking for her?" Cheryl asked.

The chief nodded. "For several hours. We thought the same thing you did. That she just ran away. But we couldn't find her. Talked to her boyfriend, Warren Pope, but he hasn't seen her. Has no idea where she is."

Although Cheryl hated to say it, she asked, "What about Douglas Powell? *If* someone else was involved in her disappearance, he'd be my first suspect."

"Went by his place first thing. He was home. No sign of Joni." The chief shook his head. "We're not rulin' him out at this point, mind you. I agree that he's a person of interest. But..."

Cheryl felt Levi tense next to her. The chief's hesitation made it clear why he was here.

"You surely do not suspect Anton," Levi said, his face pale. "This cannot be happening again."

"I don't like it any more than you do, Levi," the chief said. "But I don't have a choice in this matter. I have to follow all leads. I was told that Anton showed inappropriate attention to Joni. I'm gonna have to talk to him."

"Inappropriate attention?" Cheryl said. "Who in the world told you that?"

"Warren Pope. He said he witnessed it in your shop. Is that true or not?"

"Well there was inappropriate behavior but..."

"No buts, Cheryl. Either he did or he didn't act inappropriately with her."

"There *are* buts, Chief," Cheryl insisted. "Warren broke up with Joni because of Douglas. So, Joni decided to flirt with Anton to make Warren jealous. Anton didn't act inappropriately at all. He didn't do anything to encourage Joni. The inappropriate attention came solely from Joni."

"Is this what you believe, Levi?" the chief asked him.

He nodded. "Joni was flirting with Anton. He did not return her attention."

"I understand Joni offered to visit Anton at your house out there," the chief said. He cocked his head toward the dawdy haus.

Cheryl sighed. "She offered to bring him some dessert, but I told her no. I brought it home with me and gave it to him myself that evening. Look, Chief, you have to believe us. Anton had nothing to do with Joni's disappearance."

As soon as the words left her mouth, Cheryl remembered watching Anton leave the night before. The shock of that memory made her feel dizzy for a moment. She reached out to grab the back of her couch to steady herself.

Levi took her arm. "Are you all right?" he asked.

She tried to smile. "Fine. Sorry. This is just very upsetting."

"Is Anton back there now?" the chief asked.

"I am certain he is," Levi said. He turned to Cheryl. "You stay here. I will go with the chief."

"I need to speak to you," she whispered to Levi.

"I will talk to you later," Levi said, frowning. "First we must allow the chief to reassure himself that Anton had nothing to do with Joni's disappearance."

Although Cheryl wanted to tell Levi about Anton leaving last night, she couldn't say anything in front of the chief. He would probably find it suspicious. The last thing she wanted to do was to throw suspicion toward Anton. She was certain he'd had nothing to do with Joni.

"All right," she said, letting go of Levi's arm.

Behind her, Rebecca began to fuss. "Mama, Mama, Mama, fog," she said.

"Excuse me, Chief," Cheryl said. "It sounds like Rebecca's lost her stuffed frog."

"Certainly," the chief said with a smile. "We can take it from here."

He and Levi turned and walked out the door. Officer Spencer followed them.

Cheryl scooped up Rebecca and carried her into her bedroom where she found her green stuffed frog under the crib. She retrieved it and handed it to the happy toddler. Rebecca loved her stuffed animals and her dolls. When one went missing, she knew it immediately and would fuss until it was recovered.

As her little girl played with her frog, Cheryl went into the kitchen and poured another cup of coffee. What was she going to do? She had to tell Levi that Anton had been out last night. She walked to the kitchen window and looked out. Levi, the chief, and Anton were on the front porch talking. Anton looked upset. He nodded at something the chief said and pulled the front door open. The chief and Officer Spencer went inside. Levi and Anton stayed outside on the porch. They seemed to be having a very animated discussion. Anton was gesturing wildly. Whatever Levi was telling him didn't seem to be helping. Finally, Anton took a step back and seemed to calm down. What could they be talking about?

Cheryl peeked in on Rebecca and found her daughter playing quietly. Then she went back into the kitchen. She felt like a spy, but she really wanted to know what was going on. The chief and Officer Spencer had come out and were talking to Anton. The chief shook hands with Anton, and then he and Officer Spencer began walking toward the house. Cheryl assumed they were headed to his car. Sure enough, she heard the car's engine start up, and they backed out of the driveway.

Anton went back into the dawdy haus, and Levi started walking toward their house. Cheryl waited until he stepped through the front door.

"What happened?" she asked as a grim-faced Levi came into the kitchen.

"Chief Twitchell asked Anton about his relationship with Joni. Of course, Anton told him there was no relationship."

"Did the chief believe him?"

Levi sat down at the kitchen table. "Of course he did, Cheryl. The chief was instrumental in bringing him back to Sugarcreek in the first place."

There was an odd tone to Levi's voice. Cheryl knew what it meant. He was concerned about something.

"What's wrong?" she asked.

"I hate to see Anton treated like a suspect... again. But..."

"But what?"

"These late-night drives concern me. What if the chief finds out?"

Cheryl came over and sat down next to him. "You know about his leaving last night?"

Levi frowned at her. "Ja. Do you?"

Cheryl nodded. "Yes. He certainly doesn't have to stay in the house all the time, but I have to admit that it concerned me a little bit. I was going to talk to you about it."

"Cheryl, there is nothing wrong with wanting to see your town at night. Especially if you're Anton."

"What do you mean by 'seeing your town at night'?"

Levi leaned back in his chair and sighed. "Anton has been driving around at night. Looking over his old homestead, the school, places where he used to spend time. At night, there is no one around to see him. To judge him. Even though we visited several of these places the other day, it was not enough for him. He misses his home. It is understandable, is it not?"

"Of course it is, Levi," Cheryl said. "But I'm afraid the chief might see it differently. What if someone saw him? I think Anton needs to tell Chief Twitchell about his... excursions."

Levi's eyes grew wide. "I am not sure he should. It might make him look guilty, and he is not."

"I know that, Levi," Cheryl said soothingly. "I just don't want him to come under suspicion... again. If someone else tells the police they saw him out the night Joni went missing, wouldn't it be worse? The chief would think Anton was trying to hide something from him."

Levi sighed. "You may be right. I do not know. The funeral is in a little over an hour. I do not want to discuss this now. I will think about what you have said. I just pray news of this situation does not reach anyone attending today. I believe it would be too much pressure for Anton to bear. Seeing his sister after all this time and having people whisper that he had something to do with Joni's disappearance... It is the past happening again. I cannot believe it."

"Look, we'll stand with him. Together. This time you won't have anything to feel guilty about, okay?"

Levi nodded absentmindedly.

Cheryl double-checked to make sure she'd packed everything Sharon would need before they dropped Rebecca off. But as she got Rebecca ready to go, she couldn't help thinking that two girls disappearing around Anton was more than troubling. Although she was convinced he was innocent, she had to admit that it certainly looked bad.

CHAPTER TWENTY-SEVEN

After dropping Rebecca off with Sharon, Levi, Cheryl, and Anton headed to his sister's house for the funeral. They stopped off at a local store on the way so Cheryl could buy some rolls for the funeral dinner.

Anton had been silent ever since they'd left home. Levi had tried to reassure him that everything would be okay, but Anton's only response had been a grunt. It was evident he was nervous. His face was tight, and he kept drumming his fingers on the door handle.

Cheryl searched for the right words to say, but she couldn't find them. No matter what she came up with, she thought it sounded trite. Or insincere.

They were only about a mile away from Meredith's when Anton suddenly said, "Stop."

At first, Cheryl wasn't sure she heard him correctly.

"Stop. Please," he said again.

Levi slowed down and pulled the truck over to the side of the road. "What's wrong?" he asked Anton.

"I...I just can't do it." Anton shook his head slowly. "I want to go to the service, but I just can't. I feel sick to my stomach. With this girl missing...It's just like it was ten years ago. I can't abide the looks again. The stares. People believing I'd hurt a young girl."

He looked at them with tears in his eyes. "I'm sorry. I really am. Just let me out. I'll walk back to the house."

"Do not be ridiculous," Levi said. "We will not dump you off at the side of the road. If you do not want to attend your mother's funeral, we will all go home. We barely knew your mother. We were attending the funeral for you."

"Levi's right," Cheryl said. "Let's just go home."

Before Anton could respond, a buggy passed them by and then pulled over to a spot in front of them. Seth got out and walked up to the truck.

"Trouble with your truck?" Seth asked when Levi rolled down his window.

"No. Anton is not sure he wants to go to the service," Levi said. "We will probably turn around and go home."

Seth didn't say anything for a moment. He just stared down at the ground. Then he removed his large black hat. When he looked up his expression was grave. He looked past Levi and focused his attention on Anton.

"Son, you do whatever you must. We will support you. But may I ask you a question?"

"Yes, sir," Anton said.

"What is your reason for not attending the service?"

Anton inhaled sharply. "Have you heard that a young girl is missing?"

"Ja. Some friends stopped us up the road and told us."

Anton shook his head. "If I go to my mother's funeral, people will stare at me. Judge me. They'll think I had something to do with it."

"I see," Seth said. "And did you?"

"No!"

Anton's response was immediate and emphatic.

"So you will turn back because of people who choose to believe a lie? People who are not your friends? Are these people's opinions more important than saying goodbye to your maam?"

Anton was quiet for a moment. Then he said, "No, sir. They're not."

Seth put his hat back on and went back to his truck. As he pulled his buggy out onto the road, Levi looked at Anton.

"What do you want me to do?" he asked.

"Let's go."

"Home or to the funeral?"

"To the funeral." He gave Cheryl and Levi a tight smile. "Please stay close to me while we're there. You may have to hold on to me. I could bolt at any second."

Cheryl laughed softly. "I don't believe that. You'll be fine."

"Of course, if I start to chicken out you could just have your father talk to me, Levi. I remember him giving me good advice when I was younger. It's too bad I didn't listen better."

"He always believed in you, Anton," Levi said.

Anton put his head down. "I know," he said.

Levi started the truck up and headed down the road, passing his parents. He waved at them, and they waved back. Cheryl could see Elizabeth in the back. Esther was at the store, and Eli was running the petting zoo and corn maze.

As they approached Meredith's, they saw buggies parked all around the two-story white house. Levi pulled up next to the barn where several other cars and trucks had been parked.

Anton's complexion was ghostly white, but he opened the door and stepped out. Cheryl shot Levi a look, and he gave her a slight nod. After locking the truck, he joined Anton, who was staring at the house.

"Are you ready?" Levi asked.

"I . . . I guess so," he answered shakily. "Let's get this over with."

They started toward the front porch when someone called Levi's name. They turned to see Seth, Naomi, and Elizabeth hurrying toward them.

"Wait for us," Naomi called out. "We'll go in together."

Cheryl felt tears spring to her eyes. She was so blessed to be a part of this wonderful family. Even though Naomi had originally expressed some doubts about Anton, here she was, supporting him, her son, and her daughter-in-law.

They caught up to them, and the entire group continued together toward the house. Several people stood on the porch, and conversation stopped as they approached. Naomi acted as if everything was normal and said hello to the people she knew.

They entered the house and found Ada's coffin in the middle of the living room. Cheryl heard Anton's sharp intake of breath. He had to know she would be displayed since it was the custom for Amish funerals.

Levi put his arm around Anton and went with him to the coffin. Cheryl and the rest of the Millers waited until they'd moved on and then filed past. Cheryl didn't actually look at Mrs. Birken since she'd never known her. It seemed intrusive.

They moved on to the large dining room, which had been emptied of furniture. Chairs and benches had been lined up for those attending the service. The Amish treated a funeral like a church service. There would be a sermon. Maybe two. Some singing. A few words about the deceased. Then some would go to the cemetery for the burial while others stayed to eat the food that had been brought by the community. Seth, who was carrying a large casserole dish, took it into the kitchen for Naomi. He also took Cheryl's bag of rolls. The rest of the family found seats. The men sat on one side of the room and the women on the other. Naomi, Cheryl, and Elizabeth were able to sit together. Seth came out of the kitchen and joined Levi and Anton.

Just as it had happened outside, conversation came to a halt as people saw Anton taking a seat. When talk resumed, it was in whispers. Although Cheryl acted as if she hadn't noticed, she was certain Anton had. Although no one would be rude or confront him directly, the atmosphere was distinctly uncomfortable. Obviously, the news about Joni had spread to the Amish community.

A few minutes later, a woman walked into the room. She looked to be in her late thirties or early forties with dark hair and features that reminded Cheryl of Anton. Naomi nudged her, confirming that this was Meredith. Several people went up to her, probably offering their condolences.

Meredith spoke to them and smiled. At one point, her eyes scanned the room. Her gaze stopped when she saw Anton. The smile left her face, and her lips thinned. She quickly looked away, but it was obvious she was upset.

Cheryl couldn't help but think about her brother, Matt. They'd had their difficulties, but they'd worked through them. They had a great relationship now. Matt's wife was pregnant and Cheryl would soon be an aunt. She could hardly wait. She suddenly felt sad for Anton. Naomi had told her that Meredith was married and had three children. Anton didn't know his nieces and nephews, and they didn't know him.

Since it was almost ten o'clock, people began taking their seats. Some of the men stood in the back so that everyone would have a place to sit.

A man came up and led everyone in two hymns. After that, one of the Amish elders took his place and began to speak. He mentioned Ada, the kind of person she was, emphasizing her devotion to God. Then he continued on to his sermon. Not a lot of praise was heaped on the deceased, because the Amish felt it could get close to pride.

The elder talked about living a life for God, which meant putting Him first and serving others. It was a typical sermon delivered in the Amish church. The Amish took helping their neighbors very seriously. There weren't any Amish on welfare. The community cared for its own. Seth and Naomi were primary examples of charity and love. Cheryl felt other churches could learn from the Amish in this regard. The elder also read extensively from the Bible.

After the first sermon ended, the congregation sang two more songs and another elder continued reading from the Bible.

At the end, he also said a few words about Ada. He encouraged those attending to offer assistance to her family. And then it was over.

Everyone stood up, and the room began to empty from the back. Naomi was staying to help serve food, so she and Seth weren't going to the cemetery. Cheryl, Levi, and Anton headed toward the front door so they could join the procession to the burial.

They had just stepped outside when a man approached them. Cheryl realized it was Joel Hostettler. She hadn't noticed him inside the house and had assumed they hadn't come.

"You have no business coming here," he said loudly, sticking his finger in Anton's face.

Anton tried to walk past him, but Joel blocked his path. "You are an evil man who was not satisfied taking the life of one girl. Now you have taken another one."

"I did not hurt Liesel," Anton said quietly. "And I had nothing to do with Joni's disappearance." He looked into Joel's eyes. "I'm so sorry about Liesel, but I didn't hurt her. I never would have done anything to cause her harm. Never. I wouldn't hurt anyone, Joel. I'm sorry if you don't believe me, but I can't help that. Now please let us pass."

"I will not," he roared. "Not until you admit what you did."

"I didn't do anything," he said. "I didn't hurt Liesel."

"You are a liar," Joel said. "You wrote her a note. You asked her to meet you at the Noffsinger house."

"I didn't write that note, I swear. It wasn't sent by me."

Joel took a step closer to Anton, his expression full of rage.

Levi moved in front of Anton and for a moment, Cheryl wondered just what her nonviolent husband intended to do. Before she had a chance to find out, a voice spoke loudly from behind them.

"Leave my brother alone, Joel."

They turned around to see Meredith Kirchner looking daggers at Joel.

Chapter Twenty-Eight

J oel looked like someone had slapped him in the face although no one had laid a hand on him. A couple of Amish men came up next to them. Cheryl assumed one of them was Meredith's husband. She was right.

"I believe my wife asked you to walk away from her brother," he said firmly. "I know you will honor her request since today is her mother's funeral."

Joel seemed confused for a moment, but finally, he turned and walked down the steps, stomping toward a buggy where his wife waited. She didn't look at him as he climbed inside and picked up the reins. She seemed embarrassed. The Amish were not confrontational. She was probably humiliated by her husband's actions.

Anton looked confused as he stared at his sister. "Meredith?" he said.

Meredith's body shook as she stared back at her brother. "We have our differences, Anton, but that man will not accuse you of something so terrible while he is on my property."

"Th-thank you," he said, clearly emotional. "Can we talk?"

She shook her head. "Not today. My attention is on our mother. I am certain she would have rather had you show up while she was still alive."

"I know. I'm sorry. I didn't think either of you wanted to see me."

"Not want to see you?" Meredith said, her voice high. "I have wanted to see you for ten years. Walking away from your family is never the answer, Anton."

"I want to explain..."

"There is no good explanation." Meredith sighed. "I am grateful you came today. I have heard you are staying with the Millers?"

"Yes, in their dawdy haus."

"I will contact you tomorrow." She turned and headed back into her house. Her husband stayed behind.

"Abel Kirchner," he said, holding his hand out to Anton, who shook it. "She was praying you would come. I believe the rift between you can be mended with a little effort. Perhaps you can stay in town until you have the chance to speak together."

"Thank you, Abel," Anton said, wiping his eyes. "I'll stay until we can talk."

"Good. I will let her know. I am sure you will be hearing from your sister." Abel turned and went into the house.

Levi took Anton's arm and led him off the porch. "If you want to follow the cars to the cemetery, we need to get in line," he told Anton.

"I've changed my mind," Anton said. "I'm exhausted, and I don't think I can take any more of this right now. Do you mind?"

Levi shook his head. "Of course not. It is up to you."

"Thank you. Thank you both so much."

They all walked over to Levi's truck and got in.

"You were planning to leave tomorrow," Cheryl said. "Are you able to stay a bit longer?"

Anton smiled. "To make amends with my sister? I can stay as long as it takes." The smile on his face suddenly faded. "I'll look for another place to live during that time. I'm sure you weren't planning on me being with you for so long. I certainly don't want to be an imposition."

"You are not an imposition," Levi said. "We are happy to have you stay with us."

Cheryl and Levi dropped Anton back at the house and then went over to the cottage to pick up Rebecca. When Sharon let them in, they found their daughter playing happily. She smiled when she saw them.

"Rebecca seems very content," Cheryl said to Sharon. "You must have made a good impression."

Sharon laughed. "I sat with her on the floor, and she introduced me to her toys. She particularly loves her Oma and her *fog*."

Cheryl laughed. "Yes, she does." She looked at Levi. "It's past lunch. Why don't we get something to eat?"

"Sounds good," he said. "Maybe we should have asked Anton if he wanted to go with us."

"He seemed tired," Cheryl said, "but why don't you call him and see if he wants to meet us someplace."

Levi hesitated a moment. "It just occurred to me that he might not want to be seen out in public right now."

Cheryl sighed. "You're right. I should have thought of that." She snapped her fingers. "Why don't we call the Honey Bee, order some food to go, and take the food to our place?"

"I believe it would be easier to eat here, ain't so?" Sharon asked. "The Honey Bee is not far. Anton could just drive over here."

"Even better." Cheryl smiled at her. "Thank you. We had a rough time at the funeral, and I'm a little rattled."

"I am sorry to hear that," Sharon said. "What happened?"

"You probably don't know that Joni, the girl who works at the Swiss Miss, has gone missing," Cheryl said.

Sharon's mouth dropped open. "No, I had no idea." She shook her head in disbelief. "Surely no one is blaming Anton for this."

"Unfortunately, some are. Including Liesel Hostettler's parents. Her father confronted Anton after the service. Blamed him for both girls' disappearances."

"That is terrible," Sharon said. "How is Anton?"

"You can imagine."

"Yes, I can," said Sharon.

"Why don't you call him, Levi?" Cheryl said. "See what he wants to eat and tell him to come over here."

"All right." Levi walked into the kitchen so he could make the call.

Sharon sat down in a chair near Rebecca, and Cheryl sat on the couch. "Cheryl, have the police questioned Douglas Powell?"

"The chief went to Douglas's house this morning, but Joni wasn't there," she said. "Even so, in my mind, Douglas is the number one suspect."

The corner of Sharon's mouth twitched. "Number one suspect? Is that how the police talk?"

Cheryl smiled at her. "Sorry. I read a lot of mysteries."

"Do not apologize. I think it is very interesting." She glanced back at Levi. "I had a cousin who used to bring some books to my house without our parents knowing. Have you ever heard of Nancy Drew?"

Cheryl grinned. "I certainly have. My mother used to read them when she was a girl. She kept them all, and I read them too."

Sharon covered her mouth with her hand as she laughed. "I found them quite entertaining," she said after she put her hand down. "But I would never tell my mother that."

"I understand." Cheryl looked toward the kitchen. Levi seemed to be taking a long time talking to Anton. She hoped he'd agree to have lunch with them. He shouldn't be alone now.

"Sharon," Cheryl said, "when Mr. Hostettler confronted Anton at the service, Anton's sister defended him. They plan to talk. I'm very hopeful they'll find a way to fix their broken relationship. Anton is staying a while longer so they can get together."

"Oh, Cheryl, I am so happy to hear that," Sharon said. Cheryl noticed tears in her eyes. She really did care about Anton.

"Maybe something good will come out of this horrible situation," Cheryl said. "Anyway, I hope so."

Levi came back into the living room. "Anton told me what he wanted for lunch. He'll head over here in a little bit. He sounded glad for the company." Levi picked Rebecca up from the floor.

"Dada, Dada, Dada..." she said before giving him a kiss on the cheek. Levi smiled and hugged her close.

Cheryl wondered if the same thing was on his mind that had been on hers all day. Fractured families. Cheryl made a silent vow that she would always value what she and Levi had with his family and hers.

Cheryl smiled at her husband and Sharon. "I'd like to stop by the store and check on Esther," she said. "She was very upset about Joni this morning and has been holding down the fort alone today. Levi, why don't you stay here and play with Rebecca? Sharon and I will pick up the food from the Honey Bee. Is that okay?"

Levi smiled. "That is fine with me."

"Do you mind, Sharon?"

She shook her head. "Not at all."

"I would like a grilled cheese sandwich and some molasses ginger cookies," Levi said.

"Okay. What does Anton want?"

"He wants the grilled chicken panini sandwich. And he made it clear he wanted to pay the bill since he'd asked us out for lunch today."

Cheryl started to protest, but Levi shook his head. "It is important to him. We'll just give him the receipt. He wants to bless us."

"All right. That's very nice of him." Cheryl looked at Sharon. "Ready?"

"Let me get my cloak," she said. "It seems to be getting colder."

As Cheryl waited, she couldn't help thinking about the runaway girl and Joni. Where were they? Were they safe? Were they out in the cold?

Cheryl prayed that God would keep them both safe.

CHAPTER TWENTY-NINE

Cheryl and Sharon went by the Swiss Miss before going to the Honey Bee. Although Cheryl usually wanted the store to be busy, she hoped today would be slow since Esther was working alone. They had other part-time helpers, but they hadn't found anyone who was available today. Some of their extra staff had been hired by other businesses to work during the festival. Cheryl had been willing to keep looking, but Esther had insisted she could handle things on her own.

"I am so glad to see you," Esther said when Cheryl walked in. "Have you heard anything about Joni?"

Cheryl shook her head. "No, but I haven't talked to the chief since early this morning. Why don't I call him and…" Before she could finish her statement, she saw the chief's car pull up outside and park. "I guess I don't need to call him after all. Maybe he has some news."

As they waited for the chief to come into the store, Esther asked about the funeral.

"Well, it was interesting," Cheryl told her. "Talk to your mother tonight. She'll tell you everything that happened."

The door to the shop opened, and the bell above it tinkled. The chief walked in. He looked worried. Cheryl was certain he was under a lot of stress.

"Hi, Chief," Cheryl said. "Have you found Joni?"

He shook his head. "No, and her parents are frantic. The weather's supposed to get rough tonight, and that just makes it worse." He nodded at Sharon. "Good to see you again," he said.

"I am happy to see you too, Chief," she said, "but I am sorry there is so much trouble in the village right now."

"I'm sorry about it too," the chief said, sighing. "This is a great place. Something like this... Well, it makes people act strangely. They get suspicious of each other. We should be banding together to find Joni, but instead, I hear nothing except accusations and suspicions."

"What do you mean, Chief?" Cheryl asked.

"Several people are convinced Anton Birken is behind Joni's disappearance. Douglas Powell points the finger at Warren Pope. Warren Pope swears it's Douglas. No one has any evidence. Just suspicions."

"And what do you think?" Sharon asked.

"I have no idea. I don't believe Anton is the kind of person to do something like this, yet he comes into town and someone goes missin' again." He blew out a quick breath. "It is becomin' harder and harder to defend him."

"Oh, Chief," Cheryl said. "Don't you think Anton would have to be one of the stupidest people in the world to come back here and snatch another girl—if he'd done something like that years ago? He might not be perfect, but he certainly isn't dumb."

He nodded slowly. "That makes good sense. Sometimes it's hard to see the big picture when there are so many people telling you what to think. Thanks, Cheryl."

"You're welcome."

"Oh, I almost forgot the reason I'm here," he said. "That runaway. I think we found her."

Cheryl's heart leapt with joy. "You did? Where is she?"

The chief looked embarrassed. "I'm sorry, Cheryl. I don't mean we actually found the girl, but we may have found out who she is."

A rush of frustration surged through Cheryl. "Oh." She sighed, trying to dismiss her disappointment. "So who is she?" she said finally.

"I believe her name is Angie Simpson. Sixteen. She lives in Columbus. Ran away three weeks ago."

"Why do you think this is her?" Cheryl asked.

"Well, she fits the description you gave us, but I'd like you to take a look at this picture. Tell me if this is the girl you saw."

The chief reached into his pocket and pulled out a photo. It looked like the kind of picture taken for school yearbooks. He held it out, and Cheryl looked at it. The girl in the photo looked happy...and clean. But she was definitely the same girl. How could a child go from this to living on the streets and stealing to stay alive?

Cheryl handed the picture back to the chief. "Yes, that's her. Do you know why she ran away?"

"Seems like her parents were talkin' divorce. Told the girl she'd need to choose which parent she wanted to live with during the school year. It was too much for her so she took off. Angie has a friend in Canton who told her she could stay at her house, but when Angie got there, she found out her parents hadn't agreed to shelter a runaway. They planned to call her parents so Angie took off again. No one knows how she ended up here, but the friend said Angie planned to hitchhike. Probably got picked up by someone driving through Sugarcreek."

Cheryl sighed. "She couldn't choose between her parents. It hurt too much."

"Yes," the chief said. "But this situation woke the parents up. Seems they're in counseling and are determined to keep their marriage together. But if we can't talk to Angie, we can't tell her that."

Cheryl heard a sound and turned around. Esther was crying softly, and Sharon was trying to comfort her.

"Oh, Esther," Cheryl said. "I'm sorry. Your friend is missing, and we're talking about another girl in trouble."

Esther shook her head. "I am not crying just because of Joni. I also hurt for Angie. I cannot imagine how hard it would be to have to pick between my maam and daed. I could not do it. How sad that her only solution was to leave home."

"You have a good heart," Cheryl said. She turned to the chief. "Do you mind if I ask what you've done to find Joni?"

"I sent some officers to pick up Douglas Powell," he said. "I want to talk to him again. Find out where he was last night. It seems that Joni's parents found her room empty about ten o'clock. They believe she snuck out of the house, but what happened after that is anyone's guess."

Esther cleared her throat and wiped her eyes with a tissue Sharon had given her. "Chief, Joni told me once that sometimes she sneaks out of her window to see her boyfriend, Warren Pope."

The chief's eyebrows shot up. "Now that's interesting. I talked to him once. Sounds like we need to have another meetin'."

"But she always went home after seeing him," Esther said. "It is not like her to stay out late. Their meetings were always short. Joni was afraid her parents would check her room and find her gone."

"Maybe something else happened last night," Cheryl said. "Something unexpected."

"Possibly." The chief sighed. "Two missin' girls at one time. Seems odd."

"Just a coincidence, Chief," Cheryl said. She couldn't help thinking that there were actually three missing girls. What had happened to Liesel Hostettler? Would her parents ever know? She was struck by the similarities between the night Liesel went missing and Joni's situation. Seems both girls had escaped through their bedroom windows.

The chief sighed. "I'd better get goin'. Need to question Douglas and check up on Warren." He frowned at Cheryl. "I may have to talk to Anton again. No matter how I feel about his innocence, I have to treat him like any other suspect."

Cheryl nodded. "I know that, Chief." She felt bad for not telling him about Anton not being home when Joni went missing. It looked like she and Levi would have to confront him about it. If Anton wasn't willing to tell the chief the truth, they would have to. Keeping it secret wasn't right.

"I'll let you know as soon as I find out somethin'," he said. "I know you're worried about Joni."

"I'd also like to know if you find Angie," Cheryl said. "It's supposed to storm tonight. I worry that she'll be out in it."

"This girl chose to run away, Cheryl. Don't start blamin' yourself for her situation. It isn't your fault." He swung his gaze toward Esther and Sharon. "I don't think I've ever known anyone so willing to take responsibility for whatever goes wrong. You two need to reassure her that not everything bad that happens in the world is her fault."

"Ja, you're right, Chief," Esther said. "We will do what we can."

"And I will help," Sharon said.

Cheryl sighed in frustration. "I'm standing right here, you know. And I don't think everything is my responsibility. But this might be. I shouldn't have chased Angie. I should have watched her and called you, Chief. If I had, she might be safe and sound today."

The chief folded his arms across his chest and stared at Cheryl with a disapproving look. "You do realize that when we find her we can't just pack her up and send her home, right? She's a thief and will have to face charges. She won't get off scot-free."

Cheryl shrugged. "I realize there will be consequences, but surely because of her situation you can work something out."

The chief grunted. "Sure. I'll just tell everyone she stole from that she's had a tough time. We should just cut her some slack." He shook his head. "Let's find her first. We'll talk about what happens next after that."

He tipped his hat and left.

"I believe we should pray," Sharon said softly, after the chief was gone.

The three women held hands and prayed for Joni and Angie, that God would keep them safe and find a way to return them to their parents.

CHAPTER THIRTY

After leaving the Swiss Miss, Cheryl and Sharon went across the street to the Honey Bee to order their food. When they got back to the cottage, Anton's car was there. Although Sharon tried to hide it, Cheryl noticed her checking to see if her hair was still neatly tucked into its bun under her kapp.

As soon as they pulled in the driveway, Levi came out to the car to help carry the food bags. He smiled at Cheryl as she got out of the car. "I think our daughter has fallen in love. I realize she is very young, but it seems Anton has captured her heart."

When they walked into the house, Cheryl saw immediately what Levi was talking about. Anton was on the floor with Rebecca, who was putting her frog on top of his head. She laughed hysterically when Anton made frog sounds.

"Ribbit, ribbit," he'd say in a froggy voice, which caused Rebecca to go into gales of laughter. Cheryl had to laugh along with her.

Rebecca waved at her mother when she came in. "Mama, Mama, Mama…" she said. Then she reached over and took the frog off Anton's head. This time she put a stuffed dog on his head. Anton began to bark and paw like a dog. Once again, Rebecca laughed with abandon.

Levi leaned over close to Cheryl. "This has been going on for quite some time. Our daughter does not tire of it, and Anton has the patience of Job."

"He will make a wonderful father someday," Sharon said softly.

Cheryl turned her head to look at Levi. Sharon couldn't see her raised eyebrows. "Maybe we need to serve lunch," she said.

"Sounds like a good idea," he said.

He carried the bags over to the table, and Cheryl began to divide the food. Then she poured glasses of tea for everyone. When it was ready, she asked Levi to put Rebecca in her high chair. She was glad they'd kept an extra one at the cottage. Rebecca began to fuss and point at Anton.

"I think Rebecca would like to sit next to you," Levi said. "Do you mind?"

Anton smiled. "A resident of Sugarcreek who actually likes me? I would be honored. But first, I'd like to reimburse you for the meal."

Cheryl got the receipt and gave it to him. "You really don't need to do this," she said.

"But I want to." He looked at the receipt, took some cash from his wallet, and handed it to her.

"Thank you, Anton," Cheryl said. "That's really nice of you."

"It's nothing compared to everything you've done for me. Now where do you want me?"

Levi gestured to the chair next to Rebecca's high chair, and Anton sat down. Rebecca giggled with delight.

As they ate their lunch, Cheryl told about her meeting with the chief. "I can't imagine where Joni is," she said. "Or Angie. My mind keeps going back and forth between them. One girl who left home on purpose and one who may have been taken against her will."

"I still can't believe anyone would think I could actually kidnap and hurt another human being," Anton said. "You know, I miss this town. I used to love it here. But when the people you grew up around don't trust you, when they think you're capable of terrible things…"

"I can't imagine what you went through," Cheryl said. "I'm so sorry."

"That's very kind of you to say." Anton smiled at her. "You and Levi—and your parents—have made this bearable. I don't know what I'd do without you."

"Anton, you said you were not sure what happened to Liesel," Sharon said. "May I ask why you can't be certain she didn't simply run away?"

"I want to believe that, Sharon, I really do. But the truth is, I really don't know," he answered. "Even though she threatened to leave more than once, she wouldn't have done it without telling her parents she was going away. She would have at least written them a note." He leaned back in his chair. "Liesel loved her folks. She even told me once that she wanted to make sure they knew how much she loved them. She believed once she left, she would be shunned. She'd never be able to see or talk to them again. That's why it was important they know she wasn't rejecting them. It was the Amish lifestyle she couldn't abide."

"But no one ever found a note?" Cheryl said.

Anton shook his head. "No. That's why I think it's possible something else happened. Something out of her control. I certainly hope I'm wrong."

"The police looked closely at Douglas Powell after Liesel went missing," Cheryl said. "You told us he had a crush on her?"

Anton nodded. "A big crush. He hated me because he thought there was something between Liesel and me. No matter how many times I tried to tell him there wasn't, he wouldn't listen. I finally gave up. Decided my relationship with Liesel wasn't his business. He hung around though. Followed Liesel around."

"That is disturbing," Levi said. "He has done the same thing with Joni."

"Look, I know it seems as if Douglas could be involved," Anton said. "But truthfully? I don't buy it. In his own way, Douglas really cared for Liesel." Anton frowned at Levi. "Have you noticed the similarities between Liesel and Joni?"

Levi stared at his friend for a moment, his forehead wrinkled in thought. "You are right," he said, finally. "I never thought about it. They are very similar."

"They both have dark hair, brown eyes. Even their facial features are alike."

"So he's stalking Joni because she looks like Liesel Hostettler?" Cheryl said. "That certainly doesn't excuse his actions. His behavior is still inappropriate."

"I realize that," Anton said. "But maybe it will help you to understand him better."

"I don't want to understand him," Cheryl said sharply. "I just want Joni home with her folks."

"Anton knows that, Cheryl," Levi said. "We all want the same thing."

Cheryl started to respond when a knock came at the door. Levi got up to answer it. Cheryl could hear voices and got up to see who Levi was talking to. She saw Chief Twitchell standing at the door.

"Hello, Chief," she said.

A cold gust of wind blew through the front door, and Levi shut it. The expected storm was getting closer. Something that didn't make Cheryl feel any calmer.

"Do you know where Anton is?" the chief asked.

"I'm right here," Anton said, walking out of the kitchen. "What can I do for you?"

"You can tell me the truth, for starters," the chief said gruffly.

"The truth about what?" Anton said.

"You were seen driving near Joni's house the night she disappeared. Why didn't you tell me you were out last night?"

Anton's cheeks flushed. "I should have, Chief. I'm sorry. I was afraid it would make me look guilty."

"Well, young man, you accomplished that goal," the chief said, scowling at him. "Not being honest with me was a big mistake. I'm gonna have to take you down to the station..."

The chief was interrupted by his walkie-talkie. He pressed a button on the device attached to his uniform. Although Cheryl could hear someone speaking, she couldn't make out what they said. The chief listened and then clicked the button again.

"Officer Spencer just finished talking to Warren Pope. He finally admitted that he and Joni were supposed to meet last night. He didn't go because his parents were watching him too closely."

"Meet where?" Cheryl asked.

"The Noffsinger house."

"You're kidding," Cheryl said. "The same place Liesel was supposed to meet Anton the night she disappeared?"

"Actually, it's been used before by some kids in the village," the chief said. "It's been goin' on for years. We clear it out and board it up, and a few months later we find they've broken in again. The church needs to either tear it down or sell it."

"It's really close to our house. Do you think she's there?"

"I have no idea, but I'm gonna find out right now."

"I want to go with you," Cheryl said.

"I don't think that's a good idea," Levi said.

"But Joni knows me, Levi. If she's there, she'll listen to me. The police might scare her."

"All right. I'll stay with Rebecca." His eyes suddenly widened as he looked at Sharon. "Oh. That would mean Sharon would be here with us..."

Sharon shook her head. "Please, do not be ridiculous. I am quite safe. This is an emergency. Please go, Cheryl."

"All right, if you're sure."

Sharon smiled at her. "I'm sure."

"Cheryl, I will pack up Rebecca," Levi said. "Anton and I will go to the house. That would be more proper and that way you can simply come home after you see if Joni is at the Noffsinger house."

"Perfect idea, Levi," Cheryl said with a smile. "I'll see you there." She gave Sharon a hug. "Thank you for all your help. You'd better tuck in tonight because of the storm. I'll come over tomorrow and check on you. And if worse comes to worst, there is a phone..."

Sharon smiled at her. "I know how to use a phone, Cheryl. And if it is an emergency, I will not hesitate to call you."

"Good. Levi, make sure you leave our phone numbers for Sharon before you leave."

He nodded his agreement.

"Do you mind if I come with you, Chief?" Cheryl asked. "I guess I should have asked."

"No, I agree with your thinking. You could be helpful if Joni's hiding in the house."

Cheryl grabbed her coat, and she and the chief raced out to his patrol car. Cheryl was hopeful they would find Joni, but one thing bothered her. If Warren didn't show up last night, why didn't Joni just go home? None of the answers that popped in Cheryl's head gave her comfort.

CHAPTER THIRTY-ONE

As they drove toward the Noffsinger place, the wind began to strengthen. The storm clouds above them were dark and roiling, with the growing promise of severe weather.

When the rain began, it was light, but before long it was coming down in sheets. Cheryl was concerned about Levi and Rebecca being out in this, but she knew Levi would wait it out if he needed to. He'd never take chances with Rebecca.

By the time they reached the house, the roads and fields were beginning to flood. When the chief pulled up to the front of the house, Cheryl could see that it had once been beautiful. Although the Amish kept their houses plain, the Noffsinger house still had traces of its Victorian style. A turret on one side of the house went all the way up to the second floor. Wooden scrollwork on the outside was a nod to its past beauty. Suddenly Cheryl felt sad about this beautiful old home that had been neglected and abandoned.

She pulled the hood of her raincoat up over her head as she and the chief got out and ran to the large wraparound front porch. Cheryl started toward the front door when the chief suddenly grabbed her. He pointed down, and Cheryl saw she had almost stepped in a large hole on the floor of the porch.

"Thank you," she said loudly. The rain and the wind roared around them, making it hard to hear.

He held her arm until they got to the front door. Although it was locked, the chief shoved his shoulder against it and it opened. The doorframe was rotten and couldn't resist his effort.

The lack of sunlight made it hard to see. Dust covered everything, making Cheryl sneeze. The chief put his finger up to his lips, sending her a message to be quiet. She wanted to explain to him that she couldn't help sneezing, but instead she just nodded.

Chief Twitchell took a flashlight out of his vest and turned it on. There was still some furniture in the house. Most of it was broken and shoved into the corners. He swung the flashlight around the room, but it was empty. They proceeded to the kitchen, which was vacant except for the shelves on the walls and the sink and counters. Again, nothing. They searched the entire first floor but couldn't find anyone or even signs someone had been there.

The chief started toward the stairs. "Be careful," he whispered to Cheryl. "I doubt the steps are in very good shape."

She followed him slowly upstairs. The second floor had several bedrooms. They checked the first three, which were completely empty. Then they went into the turret room.

"Look," the chief said softly.

The room had been cleaned, and there was a twin-sized mattress on the floor, covered with blankets. Someone had been here. Food wrappers were in a pile next to the bed, along with several bottles of water. But whoever had been here was gone now.

They finished looking upstairs. The chief went back to the turret room, and Cheryl followed him.

"Looks to me like she was here," he said. "But where is she now?"

"I don't understand," Cheryl said. "If she was going to meet Warren here and he didn't show up, why didn't she just leave? Why would she stay here?"

Chief Twitchell shrugged. "Hard to say, but it's likely she was here."

"Maybe..." Cheryl said.

"What are you thinkin'?" he asked.

Cheryl pointed at the food wrappers. "We found some of the same wrappers at the insurance office. Seems odd, don't you think? And why would Joni bring food if she was just meeting her boyfriend for a few hours?"

"You think this is Angie?" he asked.

"Yeah, I do. And now we've probably spooked her again."

"Maybe not. Why don't we get out of here before she comes back? I'll put some officers out here to watch for her. If she returns, we can grab her."

Cheryl nodded. "Okay."

They slowly walked down the rickety stairs. Before they left, the chief checked out the basement just in case, but it was empty as well.

As they walked out of the house, thunder pounded through the sky, shaking the porch where they stood. The chief waved his hand toward the car. Cheryl put her head down, trying to fight against the wind that pushed the rain sideways. When she reached the car, she struggled to get the door open. When she did, she fell into the seat, exhausted. The chief slid into the driver's seat, breathing hard.

"What if either one of those girls is out in this?" Cheryl gasped.

"I would say they're in trouble," he said. "We need to get you home."

"Maybe you should stay at my house until this lets up," Cheryl said. "I don't think it's safe for you to drive."

The chief shook his head. "I gotta look for those girls, Cheryl. I'll be okay. I'll call for backup. If it gets too bad, we'll call off the search. But right now, I think we need to keep tryin' to find them."

Although she was concerned about the chief's safety, she certainly couldn't argue with him. Joni and Angie wouldn't last long in this weather. It felt as if the temperature had dropped drastically since they left the cottage.

The chief started the car and drove slowly down the dirt driveway. It was a miracle they didn't get stuck. All Cheryl could do was hold on and pray they'd make it.

They were almost halfway to her house before any heat started coming out of the vents in the car. It felt so good, Cheryl pointed the one in front of her directly at her face and leaned into it.

As they got closer to the house, Cheryl was relieved to see their truck in the driveway. Somehow, Levi had made it back. Even though she wasn't sure he should have tried it, she was grateful to know he and Rebecca were home.

The chief pulled up as close as he could to the front door. "You stay safe. If we find them, I'll let you know."

"Thanks, Chief," she said. She felt grateful for his service and the protection he'd provided for her. She reached over and patted his shoulder. The chief looked surprised, but he smiled.

Cheryl forced the car door open, which wasn't easy against the wind. As she slammed it shut, the front door of her house opened and she saw Levi. He came down the steps and took her hand, pulling her inside. Then he shut the door. She felt like collapsing to the floor. She was tired, wet, and cold.

"You get out of those wet clothes," he said. "I'll make you a cup of hot tea."

"Thank you," she said through shivering lips. She was so glad the electricity was still on. The house was warm, and she began to feel the chill leave her frozen body.

As she started toward the bedroom, she realized Anton and Sharon were sitting in the living room.

"What are you doing here?" she asked Sharon.

"I hope you do not mind, but I did not feel comfortable being alone in the cottage during this storm. I will go back as soon as the storm passes."

"Oh, Sharon," Cheryl said through chattering teeth, "I apologize. I should have asked you if you wanted to come over here with us. I just wasn't thinking."

Sharon smiled. "It is not your fault that I am afraid of storms. I wish I was braver, but I have always been the kind of person who cowers under the covers when the weather is bad."

Cheryl noticed Beau curled up in Sharon's lap. She smiled. "Beau hates the thunder, but it seems your presence is keeping him calm."

Sharon smiled. "He is doing the same for me."

"Where's Rebecca?" she asked Levi.

He grinned. "Believe it or not, she is down for a nap."

"With this thunder?"

Levi nodded. "I think Anton wore her out."

"Maybe you should move in permanently, Anton. I can't remember Rebecca ever sleeping through a storm like this."

He smiled at her. "I think I had more fun than Rebecca did."

Cheryl laughed. "Excuse me while I change. When I come back I'll tell you what we found at the Noffsinger house."

She clomped toward the bedroom. Her sneakers felt like they weighed ten pounds each. She knew she was leaving a wet trail of footprints, but she didn't care. When she got to her room, she peeled the wet clothes off and pulled on dry jeans, a sweater, and a pair of thick socks. She couldn't believe how good they felt.

Then she went to the bathroom. Her hair was plastered to her head. Cheryl took a towel and dried it until she could get it to look halfway normal. Before going back to the living room, she checked on Rebecca. Sure enough, she was sound asleep. She pulled her blanket up and tucked it around her before leaving her room and closing the door.

When she came back into the living room, she found that Sharon had cleaned up her wet footprints from the floor and that Levi had brewed some tea. She plopped down in a chair near the couch and sipped her hot tea. Her outside was warming up, but the tea reached inside and brought her even more warmth and comfort. Perfect.

She looked up and realized three pairs of eyes were watching her. She smiled at them. "I'm guessing you want to know what happened with the chief."

"If you do not mind," Levi said.

Cheryl took another sip of tea just as a loud crash of thunder boomed, accompanied by a flash of lightning, which made the lights in the house flicker. She listened to see if the thunder woke up Rebecca, but remarkably, she was quiet. "I hope we don't lose our electricity," she said to Levi. "I'm just now warming up."

Levi chuckled. "First of all, if that happens, I will turn on our generator. For now, why don't I start a fire in the fireplace? I was going to do it earlier, but we haven't been home that long."

A couple of minutes later, he had a fire going that immediately began to add warmth to the room. Having a husband who'd grown up without electricity had its advantages.

When he sat down, Cheryl told everyone about her experiences at the old house.

"I do not understand," Sharon said as she stroked Beau's fur. Cheryl could hear him purring from where she sat. "So you do not think Joni was there? But that was where she was supposed to meet Warren?"

Cheryl nodded. "It's odd. I really think that after Angie fled the insurance company building, she went to the Noffsinger house. Makes sense. It's abandoned. She probably saw it as shelter. But it's not very safe, I'm afraid. Needs a lot of work."

"The Amish church on the other side of town owns it," Levi said. "They plan to pull it down."

"So where is Joni?" Sharon asked, pulling the conversation back to her previous question.

"I don't know," Cheryl said. "And it worries me. If Warren didn't show up to meet her, she should have gone right home."

"I can't believe he didn't tell someone when he heard she was missing," Anton said. "That was stupid and selfish."

"That was a sixteen-year-old kid who didn't want to get in trouble with his parents," Cheryl said. "But you're right. If he'd told someone sooner, the police would have been able to get to the Noffsinger house quicker. Maybe they would have found her."

"I have a question," Sharon said. "Do you think the girls could be together? I mean, if Joni went to the house and Angie was there…"

Cheryl frowned as she considered Sharon's question. "I don't know. Frankly, I didn't see any sign that Joni had been there, but it's not impossible. I have no idea what that might mean at this point. Angie doesn't seem to be someone who would hurt Joni." She shook her head and sighed. "I have no idea what to think. I just know we have to find both of those girls. Since they weren't at the house, they could be out in this weather."

As if emphasizing her words, another large clap of thunder shook the house. This time the electricity went out.

"Do not worry, Cheryl," Levi said. "I will start the generator."

At that same moment, someone began knocking on the front door. Whoever it was seemed frantic. Levi hurried to the door and opened it. A figure stood on the porch. At first, Cheryl couldn't make out who it was.

A female voice cried out, "Please! Help me. If we don't get her out she's going to die!"

A flash of lightning revealed Angie Simpson standing in the rain, her features twisted with fear.

Chapter Thirty-Two

Cheryl jumped up and ran toward the girl, pulling her inside. "Angie," she said. "Are you okay?"

Although it was obvious, the girl was drenched and freezing, she nodded. "She's in trouble. I couldn't get her out by myself. Please... Please help me."

"What are you talking about?" Levi said. "Who is in trouble?"

Angie shook her head, water flying in all directions. "I don't know who she is. Some girl. She fell into a big hole, and it's filling up with rain. If we don't get her out, she's gonna drown!"

"Levi, the well!" Cheryl said. "Could it be Joni?"

Levi gently pushed the girl toward Cheryl. "Take care of her," he said. "Anton, come with me."

"No way," the girl said. "I'm going with you."

Cheryl looked at Sharon. "Will you stay here and watch Rebecca?"

"Ja," she said. "Just go."

Cheryl grabbed a coat out of the closet and handed it to Angie. She'd be wet again soon, but at least it would provide some protection. Then she got her own coat.

"No, Cheryl," Levi said. "I want you to stay here."

"Levi, you might need more help than you think. We can't take a chance. We have to get her out quickly or she could die."

Although he looked as if he wanted to argue, it was clear she could be right. They had no idea what to expect. "We will have to walk," he said. "The truck would only get stuck."

"Let's go."

"I need to get some rope from the shed. Anton, will you help me?"

Anton put on his coat. Levi led everyone to the back door. He reached into a cabinet and pulled out a couple of flashlights. He handed one to Cheryl and kept the other. Then he opened the door, and they all stepped out into the storm. Levi switched his flashlight on and pointed the beam of light out into the dark. "The well is that way," he said, trying to be heard above the roar of the rain. "Cheryl, you head for the well while Anton and I get the rope."

Cheryl grabbed Angie's hand. "We need to hold on to each other," she said.

The girl didn't argue. "We have to hurry," she said. "She was barely holding her head above water."

They began making their way toward the old well. The wind was so strong, Cheryl felt like they were taking one step forward and two steps back. A few minutes later, a light shone from behind them. Anton and Levi had caught up with them. Levi had a large section of rope looped over his shoulder.

Together the four of them fought their way through the rain toward the well. The old pieces of wood used to cover the well years ago had completely splintered. Levi grabbed the pieces and flung them out of the way. Then he shone his light down into the well. Sure enough, they saw Joni's face. She was almost covered with rising water.

"Joni, can you grab this rope?" Levi yelled at her.

There was no answer.

Anton took the rope from Levi. "Tie the end around that tree," he said. "I'm going down there to get her."

"I can do it," Levi said.

Anton shook his head. "You're stronger than I am. You're going to have to pull us up. All of you."

Levi took one end of the rope and tied it tightly around the nearby tree. Anton took the other end and tied it around his waist. Cheryl was thankful that two ex-Amish farm boys were going after Joni. They knew how to tie knots that would hold.

Anton walked over to the side of the well. Then he jumped in, landing next to Joni. It was clear that the water was cold, but he seemed to ignore it. He grabbed Joni just as her face started to slip under the water. He tried to get her to put her arms around him, but she was just too tired and cold. Cheryl was sure her extremities were numb. Anton wrapped his arms around her and yelled at Levi to pull them up. All three of them pulled, trying to bring them to the top, but the weight was just too much.

"We can't do it," Levi yelled.

Anton untied himself and put the rope around Joni. "Go!" he yelled.

This time they were able to handle the weight. They got Joni up over the side, and she collapsed on the ground. Levi untied her and threw the rope back to Anton. He secured himself, and they pulled him up.

Once Anton was out of the well, Levi picked Joni up and they made their way back to the house as quickly as they could. When they got inside, Levi put Joni in a chair near the fireplace. Sharon was rocking Rebecca, who must have finally been shaken out of her nap by the thunder. Cheryl grabbed a comforter from their bed and wrapped it around Joni. Then she made Angie take off her coat. She pulled her over to a spot in front of the fireplace and gave her a quilt to warm her up.

"I will get that generator going," Levi said, his teeth chattering.

Cheryl knew he was cold and wet, but they needed to raise the girls' body temperatures to keep them from developing hypothermia.

In the meantime, Anton added some logs to the fire. The living room was remarkably warm even though the rest of the house was cold. Cheryl ran to find her cell phone. Joni needed to get to the hospital as quickly as possible. Cheryl had noticed that her right foot was twisted. It was possible she'd broken her ankle when she'd fallen into the well. Unfortunately, Cheryl couldn't get a signal on her phone.

A few minutes later, the lights flickered back on. Levi trudged through the back door. Cheryl could tell how tired he was.

"Levi, we've got to get Joni to the hospital," she said. "I can't get a signal on my phone. What can we do?"

"I suppose we will have to try to make it in the truck," he said. "We have no choice."

"Let me get her out of these wet clothes first," Cheryl said. "Can you warm up the truck?"

He nodded and went out the front door.

Cheryl patted Angie's shoulder. "I think you need to come with us," she said. "You may need medical help too."

"I'm...I'm fine. Just really cold," the girl said.

"Let's play it safe, okay? Follow me, and I'll find something warm for you too."

"That sounds wonderful. I would really like to get these wet clothes off."

"Maybe you can help me with Joni. You saved her life, you know."

Angie gave her a small smile. "I'm just glad you were here."

"I am too."

Cheryl and Angie helped Joni into the bedroom. Sure enough, Joni couldn't put weight on her right foot. She cried out in pain when she tried to walk on it. She still wasn't talking but at least she was conscious and seemed to understand what was going on.

It took Cheryl a few minutes to find clothes for the girls. She had two pairs of sweatpants that she liked to sleep in. She combined them with a couple of sweatshirts. After helping them take off their wet shoes and put on socks, Cheryl found slippers they could wear. They were sturdy and would keep their feet warm.

As Angie dressed, Cheryl asked her about Joni. "How did you know where she was?" she asked.

"I didn't. I saw you guys coming to the house so I got out of there. I was running through the field, trying to find a place to hide. I heard her yelling." She shook her head. "I couldn't believe it. How did she get in there?"

"I have no idea," Cheryl said, "but my guess is that she was going to meet her boyfriend last night. They were supposed to meet in the house where you've been hiding. She cut across our land to get to the house and fell into the well. We planned to cover it, but just hadn't gotten around to it. We didn't think anyone would be out there, so we weren't that worried about it." She shook her head. "If you hadn't found her..."

"You know, it's like it was meant to be. Like I was supposed to be there at that moment."

"I believe you're right," Cheryl said. "Even when we've gotten off track, God can use us to do great things."

"Yeah, that's right." Angie's smile warmed Cheryl's heart.

"Look, we don't have long to talk right now," Cheryl said, "but I have to tell you something. Your folks have been worried sick about you. And they've changed their minds about splitting up. I guess losing you made them think about what was really important. You shouldn't have run away from home, but it looks like everything's going to turn out all right."

Tears ran down the girl's face. "I prayed, you know. Wow. When God answers, He really answers, doesn't He?"

Cheryl couldn't hold back a laugh even though she had tears in her eyes too. "Yes, He certainly does."

Cheryl quickly changed her clothes, and they all went back out into the living room. Levi and Anton were waiting. Although Cheryl felt the men needed to get out of their wet clothes too, she knew they wouldn't take the time. It was useless to argue. They were focused on getting Joni to the hospital as soon as possible.

"I think her ankle might be broken," she told Levi. "You're going to have to help her stay off of it."

"All right."

They were on their way to the front door, Joni being supported by Levi, when their front windows filled with blue flashing lights. Cheryl pulled the curtains back and saw a police car outside. The car door opened, and Chief Twitchell stepped out. He made his way to the front porch, and Cheryl let him in.

"Sorry about this," he said as he came inside. "My patrol car has been stuck in the mud for the last hour..." He stopped talking when he noticed the girls. "What in the world?" he said, his eyes wide with surprise.

Cheryl told him about Angie coming to them for help and Joni's rescue.

"We need to get Joni to the hospital as quickly as possible," Cheryl told him. "I think she's suffering from hypothermia, and her ankle might be broken. How bad are the roads?"

"Impassable for our cars," he said, "but I think an ambulance could make it. They're made to get through difficult terrain." He pressed the walkie-talkie on his shoulder. "Send a bus to..." He looked at Cheryl, who told him their address. The chief repeated it. "And let Joni's parents know we've found her. She's going to the hospital, but she's okay. And Delores, notify the PD in Columbus that we've also got Angie Simpson."

A voice came back over the walkie. "Did you just say you also found Angie Simpson, Chief?"

"That's affirmative," he said with a smile. "Now get that ambulance here. Now."

"Yes sir, Chief!"

It wasn't until Levi put his arms around her that Cheryl realized she was crying.

Chapter Thirty-Three

Cheryl woke up later than normal on Saturday. The rain had stopped, and the roads were clearing off. Thankfully, the ambulance had made it to their house and gotten Joni and Angie to the hospital. According to the chief, Joni was finally talking. She'd been upset with her parents, especially since they'd told her she couldn't see Warren. She'd called him and arranged to meet him at the Noffsinger house. Of course, Warren didn't go. As Cheryl had suspected, on the way to the house, Joni had cut across the Millers' property. She was looking at her phone and didn't notice the old well. She fell in, breaking her ankle when she landed. She'd spent the night and almost an entire day trying to get out. Then the rain started. Joni was convinced she was going to die.

The circumstances that led to Joni being rescued from the well were almost unbelievable. If Cheryl hadn't chased Angie from the insurance building, she wouldn't have gone to the old house. If Angie hadn't run from the house when Cheryl and the chief showed up, she wouldn't have found Joni. The entire thing was so miraculous that Cheryl could only thank God for the way everything turned out. She knew His hand was in it.

Joni told her parents how Anton risked his own life to save hers. Not only were they grateful, but they were telling everyone

224 | Sugarcreek Amish Mysteries

they knew that Anton was a hero. To say his reputation in Sugarcreek improved was an understatement.

Angie's parents were contacted and immediately headed to Sugarcreek. They'd stayed the night at the hospital. Angie was fine, just needed to rest. Her crime spree would have to be dealt with, but most of the merchants she stole from were refusing to press charges. Cheryl was one of them. She was hopeful the rest would join her once they understood the circumstances and found out that Angie's unselfish actions had saved Joni's life. If that didn't happen, Chief Twitchell was fairly confident they'd accept a plan to pay back the value of the goods stolen. Sharon had returned Cheryl's money, and they agreed to give the quilt to Angie as a gift. No one really wanted to see Angie go through any more trauma.

Cheryl rolled over and stared at the ceiling. She still wasn't sure what was going to happen with Anton and Sharon. Neither one of them seemed willing to leave town. Anton was spending time with his sister today. Cheryl glanced at the clock next to her bed. Nine o'clock. She couldn't believe it. She never slept this late. Where was Levi? Why hadn't Rebecca cried? She was starting to get out of bed when Beau jumped up on her chest and stared at her, causing her to laugh.

"Yes, I know I should be up now," she said. "Thanks for checking on me."

Beau leaned down and rubbed his face on Cheryl's neck. "I love you, you silly cat," she said. She ran her hand down his back, and he purred loudly. After a couple of minutes, Cheryl sighed. "We'd better get going, Beau. Have you eaten?"

Usually those words would send him scrambling for his bowl, but he just settled down as if he were getting ready for a nap.

Cheryl picked him up and put him on the bed. "Let's go find out where everyone is, okay?" She got up, slid her slippers on, and headed for the kitchen. She found Levi and Rebecca eating breakfast.

"My goodness," she said. "Why didn't you wake me?"

"You needed your sleep," Levi said. "I decided to feed Rebecca and make you some breakfast."

"You made me breakfast? Seriously?"

Levi went over to the oven. He grabbed an oven mitt and took out a plate. "I kept it warm so you could sleep as long as you wanted." He put the plate on the kitchen table. Scrambled eggs, sausage, hash browns, and toast.

"Wow. You made all of this?"

"Well, the hash browns are the kind you heat up in the toaster. But I made the rest of it."

"It looks great. Smells better," Cheryl said with a smile. She sat down at the table while Levi poured her a cup of coffee. "I feel like a queen."

"You are *my* queen," Levi said. He kissed her on the head as he put the coffee next to her plate.

"So Anton's at his sister's?"

Levi nodded. "He was really nervous."

"I'm sure Meredith has heard about Joni. I hope that makes it easier."

"I do not believe Meredith ever thought Anton harmed Liesel—or Joni. I think she was hurt because he left her and their mother behind."

"Meredith said something about that at the funeral," Cheryl said. She stuck her fork into her scrambled eggs and put them in her mouth. Delicious. "I think you should cook more often."

"With everything you've been through, it's the least I can do."

"Heard anything about how Joni's doing this morning?"

Levi shook his head. "No, but I suspect we will get an update when we go to the hospital."

"I really want to get there before Angie and her parents leave." She took a sip of coffee and then put the cup down. "I hope all the charges will be dropped against her."

"Would that be right though, Cheryl? I tend to believe there should be some consequences for her actions. She needs to learn from her mistakes."

"I know what you're saying," Cheryl said. "I just… Well, I think she was so upset she acted in a way she wouldn't normally."

"I do not know if stealing should be ignored." Levi smiled at her. "You have a very soft heart. We will have to let the chief figure out what will happen next."

"You're right." She reached over and stroked Rebecca's hair. When Cheryl pulled her hand away, she laughed and held it out for Levi to see. "She has scrambled eggs in her hair, Levi."

He shook his head. "I thought I got it all. I have to admit that breakfast was rather… messy. I cleaned up everything else."

"You're my hero."

"Thank you."

"Did you feed Beau?"

"Yes. Why? Did he try to tell you I forgot him?"

"No, actually, he was quite complimentary."

Levi smiled. "Good. At least someone in this family appreciates me. I think our daughter would rather have your eggs."

"Well, I don't know why. Yours are wonderful." Cheryl jabbed another forkful of eggs and stuck them in her mouth. She was so hungry she didn't care if they were a little dry. They tasted like ambrosia.

After breakfast, Cheryl got dressed and they left for the hospital. They took Rebecca to Seth and Naomi's since children weren't allowed in patient rooms.

After arriving at the hospital, they looked for Joni's room. When they found it, Cheryl was thrilled to see that she was awake and looked so much better. She smiled at them when they walked in.

"How are you feeling?" Cheryl asked.

"Great," Joni said. "My ankle is pretty sore, but it will improve." She pointed at her foot, which was in a cast up to the middle of her leg. "I don't think I'm going to enjoy this though."

"But it will help your ankle to heal," Cheryl said. "You need to take care of it."

"I won't be able to work for a while. Maybe several months."

"That's okay. Your healing comes first."

AnnMarie Blanchard, Joni's mother, got up from the chair where she'd been sitting. She was small and had dark hair like Joni. "I would be happy to help you in the shop if you need it,

Cheryl," she said. "I've worked in retail before. I think I could be an asset."

"I really appreciate that, AnnMarie, and I'll keep it in mind, but I suspect you need to stay home with your daughter."

"I don't want Joni's bad decisions to put you at a disadvantage."

"I have other people I can call for help, but if they can't cover the store I'll let you know. Thank you so much for thinking about me."

AnnMarie's brown eyes filled with tears. "You helped save my daughter's life. I could never thank you enough."

"Other people did more than I did."

A large man walked into the room carrying two coffee cups. He smiled at Cheryl. "Hello, I'm Jerome Blanchard, Joni's father."

"This is Cheryl Miller, Jerome. She and her husband helped save our girl."

Jerome handed one of the coffee cups to his wife and put the other one down on a nearby counter. He reached out and shook Levi's hand. Then Cheryl's. "We can't thank you enough for everything you've done."

"Thank you," Levi said, "but as my wife has been telling yours—the people you should be thanking are Angie Simpson and Anton Birken. Anton jumped into the well and made sure your daughter got to safety."

"We've spoken to Angie and her parents. They're just down the hall. We haven't been able to talk to Anton yet, but we will. He's a real hero."

"Ja, he is," Levi said. "We are all glad we could be involved in finding Joni."

"I'm sorry I put everyone in that position," Joni said. "What I did was stupid."

"Yes, it was," her father said. "And we'll talk about it later. But right now, we're just glad you're okay. The hours you were gone felt like years." He choked on his words, and it brought tears to his daughter's eyes.

"I can't believe I got myself in this kind of trouble over Warren Pope." She sighed loudly.

"I take it you're not as interested in him as you once were?" Cheryl said.

"Heavens, no. That jerk could have told someone we were supposed to meet at that old house. Maybe I could have gotten out of that horrible well hours earlier."

"I know you're upset with Warren," AnnMarie said, "but let's not call him names. *Jerk* isn't a nice word."

"Sorry," Joni said.

Frankly, Cheryl thought it was pretty appropriate, but she kept that thought to herself.

"We're going to go down the hall to say hello to the Simpsons," Cheryl said. She smiled at Joni. "You take care, okay?"

Joni nodded. "I will. And thanks again, Cheryl."

Cheryl gestured to Levi. "We'd better go."

As they walked out of Joni's hospital room, Cheryl couldn't help thanking God for a happy ending to an awful situation.

Chapter Thirty-Four

Angie smiled when Cheryl and Levi came into her room. She looked great. She was actually a very pretty girl. Today she had the same smile Cheryl had seen in her school picture. The haunted look in her eyes was gone. It probably had something to do with the couple standing next to her bed.

"How are you doing?" Cheryl asked as they approached.

"Fine. Nothing a little food and rest couldn't cure." She turned to her parents. "Mom, Dad, this is Cheryl Miller and her husband, Levi. They're the people I told you about."

Angie's mom smiled at Cheryl with tears in her eyes. "We're so grateful to everyone here for finding Angie and contacting us. We were so worried."

"Angie found us, I'm afraid," Cheryl said. "As hard as she tried to stay under the radar, when she saw someone in trouble, she forgot about herself and did everything she could to help. You should be proud of her."

"We are," her father said. "But we still have some problems to deal with. We're so sorry that she took things from the people in this town. We want to make it right."

"You don't owe me anything. I think a lot of the other business owners feel the same way."

"That's very generous of you," her dad said, "but we feel Angie needs to take responsibility for her actions. We want to pay for whatever she took." He put his hand out to Levi. "I'm Fred Simpson, by the way. This is my wife, JoAnne."

Levi shook hands with Fred. "Nice to meet you," he said.

Cheryl considered what Fred had said. She would really rather just let it go, but she could understand the wisdom behind his intentions. "The most expensive thing Angie took from me was a quilt, but it's been recovered. There was some food. I'd guess it was around twenty dollars worth."

"Thank you for being honest with us." Fred reached into his wallet and took out a twenty-dollar bill. He handed it to Cheryl. She had a tough time taking it, but she did.

"I'll pay you back, Dad," Angie said.

"Yes, you will," he said. "We'll talk about that too when we get home."

Angie smiled. "You were right, Cheryl. My parents decided to work things out. They're not splitting up."

"I'm glad," Cheryl said.

"I guess we needed a wake-up call," JoAnne said. "Angie's disappearance certainly provided that. We realized our family is our number one priority." She reached over and took Angie's hand. "We're just not sure when we'll be able to go home. If she has to face charges..."

"She won't," a voice boomed from the doorway.

Cheryl turned around to find Chief Twitchell standing there. "Hello, Chief," she said.

He nodded toward her. "None of the shopkeepers want to file charges," he said. "But I do have a list of the things Angie took and the value. You need to take care of them as soon as you can."

"No charges?" JoAnne said. Her voice caught, and she covered her face with her hand while she sobbed.

"Now, honey," Fred said. "I know it's been hard."

JoAnne tried to choke back her tears. "I'm sorry," she said. "The past three weeks have been . . . awful. Now it seems everything is working out. I'm just so relieved."

"I understand," Cheryl said with a smile. "You've been through a lot." She walked over and took Angie's other hand. "I want you to know that once it's been released, Sharon Yoder, the woman who made the quilt you took, wants to give it to you. It's a child's blanket. You're to keep it for your first child."

Angie blinked back tears. "That's so nice. She doesn't need to do that."

"I know, but she wants to."

"Please thank her for me. Can I get an address so I can write to her?"

"You know, I'm not sure how long she'll be staying in Sugarcreek. Why don't you just send a letter to her in care of the Swiss Miss? I'll make sure she gets it."

"I will." She squeezed Cheryl's hand. "Thank you, Cheryl," she said. "I'll never forget you."

"And I'll never forget you," Cheryl said softly. She looked at Levi. "We'd better get going."

He nodded. "It was nice to meet you," he said to Angie's parents.

"Happy to meet you too," Fred said.

Cheryl and Levi said goodbye to the Simpsons and Chief Twitchell. Then they walked out of the hospital room.

"That turned out better than I could have ever expected," Cheryl said in the hallway, reaching for Levi's hand.

"Ja, it did. Now what?"

"Let's head over to the shop," she said. "I want to make sure everything is running smoothly."

"Are you nervous about your new helper?" Levi asked with a smile.

"Not really."

They drove over to the Swiss Miss. When they got inside, they watched as Esther trained their new employee on the cash register.

"How's it going?" Cheryl asked.

"Sharon is doing great," Esther said. "She has learned the inventory, and now I am showing her how to check out a customer."

Sharon had decided to stay on in Sugarcreek for a while. She planned to go home after the festival. Cheryl suspected that she wanted to see if anything might happen between her and Anton. They had a lot of challenges ahead if they decided to pursue a relationship. No one knew that better than Cheryl. But with God's help, they would find their way.

Anton was supposed to meet them at the shop around one, and then they were all going to lunch.

"Esther was telling me all about the festival," Sharon said. "It sounds very exciting. I heard about it from friends in Bird-in-Hand, but it seems there is much more to it than I imagined."

Cheryl frowned. "Esther, have you seen that old scrapbook my aunt kept? There were all kinds of articles and pictures of the festival down through the years. I haven't seen it for a long time."

"I know exactly where it is," Esther said with a smile. "I found it while organizing the basement."

"You organized the basement?" Cheryl shook her head. "Wow. You really are a whiz."

Esther smiled. "I will get it." She walked away, leaving Sharon with Cheryl and Levi.

"So are you enjoying this?" Cheryl asked.

"I really am," Sharon said. "I like meeting people, and everyone is so nice."

"I suspect your mother misses you."

Sharon nodded. "Ja, she does, but I will be home soon. This is an adventure, and she is happy that I am having fun."

"Fun?" Levi said. "You think the past week has been fun?"

Sharon smiled. "Perhaps the word I should have used was...exciting."

Cheryl laughed. "Well, it was that."

Esther came back into the room holding a large scrapbook. "Is this is the one you mean?" she asked Cheryl.

"Yes, that's it," Cheryl said with a smile. "I haven't seen it in such a long time."

Esther came over and put it on the counter. Just as she did, a customer came in the door. "Excuse me," she said. She left to see if they needed help.

Cheryl opened the book and began to show the clippings to Sharon and Levi.

"I have never seen this," Levi said. "How many years of articles are in here?"

"I'm not really sure," Cheryl said. "Maybe twenty? Every time I came to visit, Aunt Mitzi would show me this book. Tell me about the festival."

As she flipped through the pages and showed them to Sharon and Levi, she reached a page with articles and pictures from eleven years ago. There was a list of events and photos of people attending some of them.

"Look there," Levi said suddenly. "There is a picture of Liesel. The photographer must have snapped the picture while she was looking his way."

As Levi pointed it out, Sharon gasped. She pulled the scrapbook closer to her and stared at Liesel's picture. Then she looked up at Cheryl and Levi, her eyes wide. "I know where Liesel Hostettler is," she said.

CHAPTER THIRTY-FIVE

After contacting Chief Twitchell, Levi called Anton and told him to get to the shop right away. The chief had just pulled up outside when Anton drove in behind him.

Cheryl had already turned over the sign on the door, closing the shop. She waited with Sharon and Levi for the two men to join them. As soon as they entered, Esther locked the front door.

"What was so important I had to run over here right away?" the chief asked. "Haven't we spent enough time together lately? You don't have any more missin' girls, do you?"

Cheryl, who was having a tough time maintaining her composure, almost lost it over the chief's question.

"No, Chief," she said, her voice trembling, "no more missing girls."

The chief walked up to the counter. "What in the world is goin' on?"

"Here." Cheryl turned the album around and pointed at the picture of Liesel Hostettler.

The chief and Anton both looked at her like she'd lost her mind.

"It's a picture of Liesel," Anton said. "I don't understand why you're showing this to us." He looked at Levi. "Why did you ask me to come over early?" He looked back and forth between Sharon, Cheryl, and Levi. "What's going on?"

Cheryl gulped several times before saying, "What's going on, Anton, is that we know where Liesel Hostettler is."

The color drained from Anton's face. "You . . . you mean her body . . ."

"No, my friend," Levi said with a smile. "Not her body. She is alive."

"You better make this a lot clearer for me," the chief said. "Right now."

Cheryl nodded at Sharon. "You tell him."

Sharon took a deep breath. "Cheryl was showing me some pictures from past Swiss Festivals. We ran across this picture of Liesel."

"So?" the chief said.

"I know her." She looked at Anton. "She lives near me in Bird-in-Hand, Anton. My mother and I buy eggs from her. Her name is Laurel Johnson."

The chief sighed and shook his head. "Just because Liesel looks like some woman you know . . . You shouldn't get people's hopes up for a flimsy reason like that. I don't want you tellin' her parents you think you know where she is."

"I have to agree with the chief," Anton said. He reached out and put his hand on Sharon's arm. "I know you mean well, but . . ."

"Will you two shush?" Cheryl said sharply. "We're not idiots." She frowned at the chief. "What if we talk to this . . . Laurel and she admits to being Liesel?"

"If that happened, I might be the happiest man in Sugarcreek today," the chief growled. "Until I tell her parents. Then I think they'd win the prize."

"We already talked to her, Chief," Cheryl said, a tear running down her cheek. "It's her. It really is."

In all the time she'd known the chief, she'd never seen him cry. Today changed that. He reached into his pocket and pulled out a handkerchief. He dabbed his eyes and Anton stared at them with his mouth open.

"But how...Why..." He seemed overwhelmed with the news.

"Look, we don't know all the details yet," Cheryl said. "We didn't stay on the phone long. She wants to talk to you, Chief. After that, she's coming here to see her parents. She left them a letter, telling them she was leaving and why. She said a friend was supposed to deliver it, but he never did. She was very upset to find out about it."

"What friend?" Anton asked. "It certainly wasn't me."

Cheryl shook her head. "I don't know. Those are questions the chief will have to ask. As you can probably imagine, we were pretty excited. Asking questions wasn't really on our minds."

The chief finished wiping his face and put his handkerchief back in his pocket. "Where's her number?"

Cheryl handed him a piece of paper with the number on it. "Please. After you talk to her, let us know what you found out. I think Anton deserves to know the truth after all these years."

The chief nodded. "Yeah, he does. And I'll tell him. But first I'll visit her parents."

"That's as it should be," Anton said.

The chief walked out of the shop with the note in his hand.

"I just can't believe it," Anton said. He stared at Sharon as if he'd never seen her before. "If you hadn't come to Sugarcreek..."

"God seems to be busy solving some very important mysteries," Cheryl said. She laughed. "This time Naomi and I weren't needed at all. I like that."

"I think you're right," Anton said. "You know, when I left the church, for the most part, I left God behind too. But after what I've seen here..." He shook his head and smiled. "I may not ever join the Amish church again, but my faith has been restored. I have my sister back, my name...For a while, I wasn't sure I should have come to Sugarcreek, but I'm so glad I did now. It was the best decision of my life."

At those words, he looked at Sharon and smiled. She smiled back at him. Seemed Anton had gained several things over the past several days, and love might just be one of them.

"Let's get lunch and head back to our house," Cheryl said. "I want the chief to be able to find us after he talks to Liesel...and her parents."

Esther opened the shop back up and Cheryl, Levi, Anton, and Sharon drove to Park Street Pizza for lunch. The pizza was incredible, but they were all too excited to eat much. They took some pizza back to Levi and Cheryl's house. While they waited to hear from the chief, Levi drove over to his parents' house and picked up Rebecca.

It was almost time for supper when the chief's car pulled into the driveway. Sharon called Cheryl's name as she started to heat up the rest of the chicken and noodles from Tuesday night. She quickly put the dish back in the refrigerator and hurried into the living room.

Rebecca was still down for a nap. The four of them waited for the chief to knock on the door. Levi got up and let him in. Sharon and Anton sat next to each other on the couch, Beau back in Sharon's lap, purring happily. Cheryl didn't have as much time with him as she used to. Running after a toddler definitely cut down on lap time. She was grateful to Sharon for showing him so much attention.

The chief walked into the room, obviously aware of the four pairs of eyes focused on him.

"Have a seat, Chief," Cheryl said. "Can I get you something to drink? A cup of coffee?"

He shook his head. "Thanks, but I don't want to get too comfortable. Shirley would like to see me get home in time for dinner tonight. Too many long days and nights lately."

"I understand." Cheryl sat down on the arm of the chair where Levi was. He put his arm around her.

"Well, you all were right, of course. Laurel Johnson is Liesel Hostettler." He sighed. "It's hard to know where to start. I guess I'll just begin with the night Liesel left town." He looked at Anton. "You're not going to be happy to hear some of this, young man. But it's time you knew what really happened."

Anton frowned. "It's all I want."

The chief took a deep breath and let it out. "The Hostettlers have some family in Sharon's hometown. Liesel had never been there, but she'd heard good things about it from her folks and others in the family. That's why she picked Bird-in-Hand. We checked with them when Liesel went missing, but none of them had any idea she was there. They'd never met her. I'm sure they'll be shocked when the news gets out. Anyway, that night, she wanted to let you know she was leavin,' Anton, but she couldn't get to you. Her parents were keepin' a close eye on her. So she asked a friend to take a message to you. To meet her later that night at the Noffsinger house."

"I never got that message," Anton said.

"No, you didn't. Douglas Powell never delivered it."

"Douglas," Anton said. "Why would he..."

The chief held his hand up. "Might as well save your indignation. You're gonna have a lot more chances to use it comin' up."

"Why didn't he tell Anton that Liesel wanted to see him?" Cheryl asked.

"Because he liked her. A lot. He showed up at the Noffsinger house that night and told her Anton wouldn't come. That he didn't want to see her anymore. He thought she might like him if she thought Anton had dumped her."

"But we weren't romantically involved," Anton said.

"Douglas didn't know that."

"But that does not make sense," Sharon said. "When Liesel and Anton talked the next time, they would know Douglas lied."

"Douglas Powell wasn't the sharpest pencil in the box back then either," the chief said. "I don't think he thought it out that much. Of course, it would have backfired, but then Liesel told him she was leaving town. He tried to talk her out of it, but she had her mind made up." He sighed again and shook his head slowly. "Not realizing she couldn't trust him, she gave him a letter. For her parents. All these years, Liesel thought her parents had read it."

"Oh my," Sharon said. "What a cruel thing to do."

"To say she was upset is an understatement," the chief said. "She assumed they knew about her decision. She never contacted them, because she assumed she was shunned. When I told her she hadn't been, she began making plans to come here and see her folks. She'll arrive sometime next week."

"But why didn't she tell them where she was going?" Cheryl asked.

"Because she didn't want the police findin' her and bringin' her back," the chief said. "Same reason she changed her name. She wasn't hidin' from her folks, she was tryin' to stay off our radar. She told everyone she met that she was eighteen. Lived on cash jobs until she was older and able to figure out how to create a new identity. Might not have worked in a bigger town, but she got away with it there."

"Wait a minute," Anton said. "This explains a lot. Except for two things. What about Douglas's alibi?"

"Douglas said he was at a party out of town. In Canton. And he was. But it was later that evening. After he met with Liesel." The chief shrugged. "There was a lot of drinking. It's possible the person Douglas used as an alibi really believed he was there the entire time. Or maybe he lied for Douglas. I have no idea."

"But what about the note? The note that I supposedly wrote?"

"That's the other thing that's probably gonna make you mad." The chief clasped his hands together. "Douglas printed that note and put it in Liesel's room. He figured that if she left without tellin' anyone except him what she was doin', when her parents found that note…"

"They'd think I did something to harm her." Anton looked stunned. "Does he really hate me that much?"

"I think he did," the chief said. "I went by and talked to him this evening before comin' over here. He's pretty broken. When he saw the way people reacted after Liesel left, he was sorry for what he did. But he couldn't fix it. He was too afraid. If it makes any difference, he kept the letter Liesel wrote to her folks. I delivered it to them earlier."

"I imagine they're elated," Cheryl said.

"Beyond that," the chief said softly. "Their daughter was just given back to them. Telling them she was alive and is coming to see them is one of the greatest privileges of my career."

"Will Douglas be charged with anything, Chief?" Anton asked.

He shook his head. "Could have maybe charged him with impeding an investigation, but since Liesel wasn't physically harmed, it wouldn't stick. Besides, it's been too long." He rubbed the back of his neck. "Douglas is probably punishing himself more than anyone else could. I think that's why he kept botherin' Joni.

She looks so much like Liesel. Maybe he thought if she liked him, somehow it meant he was forgiven."

"It will take a while for me to forgive him," Anton said.

"I understand," Chief Twitchell said. He stood.

Cheryl saw the weariness in his face. It had been a tough week for the law enforcement officer. "Thanks, Chief," she said. "For everything."

"You're welcome." He put his hat back on and headed toward the door. Before he left, he turned around and smiled at Anton. "I always knew you were innocent. Your mother would have been proud of you if only she'd lived a little longer. I know I am." He walked out the door and got into his car.

Anton seemed touched by the chief's words. "When I came back to Sugarcreek," he said, "I had no idea my life would change so much. I feel...I feel like I've found myself again. Along with some other very special blessings." He reached over and took Sharon's hand.

Cheryl smiled at them. "I think that clears up almost everything," she said. "Except for one thing."

"What's that?" Levi asked.

"The letters you sent to your mother, Anton. What happened to them?"

"I meant to tell you. As I suspected, Meredith didn't give them to her—"

"Oh, no," Cheryl said. "I'm so sorry."

"I'm not finished," Anton said with a smile. "Until about a week before she died. Meredith realized the end was coming, so she gave Maam all the letters. She read every single one before she passed away. Meri said it gave her great peace."

"I'm so glad," Cheryl said.

"I am too."

"Have you decided when you are going to leave Sugarcreek?" Levi asked Anton.

"I'll go back to Colorado next week," he said. "But then I'm coming back for good."

Levi clapped his hands together. "I am so happy to hear that."

"But there's more. I made an offer to the church for the Noffsinger house, and they accepted. I'm going to have it restored."

Cheryl could hardly believe her ears. "That lovely old house gets another chance," she said. "That makes me so happy."

"The house is not the only one getting another chance," Anton said. "I intend to spend a lot of time with my sister, her husband, and my nieces and nephews." He smiled at Sharon and gazed into her eyes. "And who knows what else might be in the future? Whatever it is, I'm looking forward to it."

Cheryl smiled at him. "I'm glad you decided to stay, Anton. Saying goodbye to Sugarcreek is hard. I know."

"Yes, it is."

At that moment, they all heard Rebecca cry. As Levi went to check on her, Cheryl went into the kitchen to finish fixing supper.

She glanced out the kitchen window and saw Ranger looking at her from the corral. Tomorrow she'd saddle him up and ride.

And life in Sugarcreek would be back to normal.

AUTHOR LETTER

Dear Readers,

Writing my last book in this series was harder than I anticipated. I was privileged to write the first book, *Blessings in Disguise*. As you can imagine, this series is close to my heart.

Over time, we've watched Cheryl Cooper's many adventures in Sugarcreek, Ohio. Her friendship with Naomi Miller grew and grew until they became best friends. And her love for a special Amish man culminated in marriage to Levi Miller and the birth of their daughter, Rebecca.

Early on, when the series began, I was able to travel to Sugarcreek and meet some of the wonderful people who live there. One highlight was getting to visit the Honey Bee Café. I originally added them to our series and was thrilled to actually meet the owner, Kathy Kimble, and all the great people who work there. If you get to Sugarcreek, stop by and tell Kathy, "Nancy says hello!"

While the series is not quite over, it is time for me to say goodbye to Sugarcreek. I found myself feeling emotional as I wrote the last scene in *Quilt by Association*. When Cheryl says to Anton, "Saying goodbye to Sugarcreek is hard. I know," the words were mine and they came from my heart.

I want to thank all of you who love this series. You make it a success. Thank you for all the comments, letters, and emails of support.

Since Guideposts has many other wonderful series to offer readers, and I'll be part of some of them, I won't say goodbye. Instead, I'll just say, *Tot ziens!* (See you later!)

Nancy Mehl

ABOUT THE AUTHOR

Nancy Mehl is a best-selling, award-winning author who lives in Missouri with her husband, Norman, and her Puggle, Watson. She's authored thirty books and, in addition to writing for Guideposts' cozy mysteries, is currently writing a new series for Bethany House Publishing. The Kaely Quinn Profiler series will kick off with book one, *Mind Games*, in December of 2018. The last book in her Defenders of Justice Series, *Blind Betrayal*, released in the spring of 2018.

All of Nancy's novels have an added touch—something for your spirit as well as your soul. "I welcome the opportunity to share my faith through my writing," Nancy says. "God is number one in my life. I wouldn't be writing at all if I didn't believe this is what He's called me to do. I hope everyone who reads my books will walk away with the most important message I can give them: God is good, and He loves you more than you can imagine. He has a good plan for your life, and there is nothing you can't overcome with His help."

Readers can learn more about Nancy through her website: nancymehl.com. She is part of The Suspense Sisters: suspensesisters. blogspot.com, along with several other popular suspense authors. She is also very active on Facebook.

Fun Fact about the Amish

The Amish are known for being community minded and self-reliant. They fund their own schools, maintain their own buildings, handle their own healthcare needs, provide assistance to those who need financial help, and even fund missions and various outreaches. Their primary means of raising funds come from benefit auctions. Auctions are prevalent throughout Ohio and Pennsylvania. Dates are easy to find with a little research.

Although a lot of these auctions focus on cattle and horses, other events offer all kinds of crafts, foods, and homemade goods. These auctions are probably best known for their beautiful quilts, and they draw people from miles around who want to take home a hand-stitched Amish heirloom.

Not only are auctions financially beneficial, the Amish use them as social gatherings. Food is usually plentiful and might include breakfast and lunch offerings—everything from biscuits and gravy to barbeque.

For those who enjoy Amish crafts and food, you'll love attending an auction!

SOMETHING DELICIOUS FROM OUR SUGARCREEK FRIENDS

Cheryl's Creamy Chicken and Noodles
(Naomi's recipe updated for the Crock-Pot)

Ingredients

1 lb. boneless chicken breasts

2 cans cream of chicken soup

2 cans chicken broth (15 oz. each)

1 stick butter or margarine

1 package frozen Reames egg noodles (24 oz.)

Directions

Put chicken on the bottom of the Crock-Pot. Pour the chicken broth and soup on top. Top with butter. Cook on low for six to seven hours.

Take the chicken out, debone and shred it, return it to the Crock-Pot.

Add the frozen noodles and cook for two more hours, stirring every 30 minutes.

Read on for a sneak peek of another exciting book
in the series Sugarcreek Amish Mysteries!

Homespun Suspicions
by Olivia Newport

*M**ake an effort.*

That's what Aunt Mitzi's note said. Cheryl Cooper
Miller still had the note, handwritten on yellow stationery, tucked
in her purse along with all the other instructions for taking on the
task of becoming a first-time property manager.

Rebecca offered a cry of protest from her stroller as Cheryl
pondered the options at the Honey Bee Café. Usually Cheryl
would fold back the hood of the stroller when Rebecca was awake
so she could see her daughter. On this Saturday morning, though,
the hood functioned as support for the welcome basket she was
transporting.

From behind the counter, Kathy Kimble pointed. "Looks like
a beautiful basket. Amish?"

Cheryl nodded. Her friend and mother-in-law, Naomi, had
directed her to the best basket weaver in the Amish church. If
she was going to make an effort, it might as well be the best
effort.

"Made up your mind yet?" Kathy said.

"Not quite."

Rebecca complained against her confinement again, and Cheryl stepped back to rock the stroller a bit and let Kathy attend to a customer whose mind was fixed. Doug, owner of the hardware store down the street, moved forward to fill the gap.

Cheryl surveyed her basket again. Aunt Mitzi's shop, the Swiss Miss, was just across the street from the café, and her cottage and home of more than forty years was a convenient four blocks down Main Street. When Mitzi answered the call to become a missionary in Papua New Guinea several years ago, Cheryl came to Sugarcreek to run the shop and live in the cottage. Now she had a husband—Levi—and a toddler daughter, and they lived on a farm of their own. It only made sense to rent out the cottage, and Mitzi had handpicked the tenant. Jayla Nuttall. Cheryl knew nothing else about her—except that apparently being her stand-in landlord would require her to "make an effort." Such an odd phrase. Cheryl wasn't unfriendly or standoffish. The Swiss Miss had thrived and even expanded to new lines of merchandise under her management. She'd made many friends in Sugarcreek among both the Amish and the Englishers. Why should she need written instruction to "make an effort"?

In a few minutes, she would meet Jayla Nuttall for the first time, and in the spirit of welcoming friendship, she would greet her with an overflowing basket representing what Sugarcreek had to offer. A book from By His Grace would hint at the caring couple who ran the bookstore. A copy of *The Budget* newspaper would introduce the warm Amish culture that surrounded Sugarcreek. A small lap quilt from the Sisters Quilt Shoppe might open conversations about what Jayla's interests were. Coupons for Yoder's Corner restaurant, the Buttons 'n Bows shop, and Get It Burger would take Jayla to places where Cheryl knew people would talk to her and make their own effort to get to know her. A gift certificate to the Swiss Miss was a given. Fresh muffins, still warm from the Honey Bee Café, seemed like just the touch to top off the basket. Cheryl checked the time and stepped to the counter again.

Doug, muffin and coffee in hand, settled at one of the tables with a newspaper.

"Ready?" Kathy said.

"I'm trying to choose something for the new tenant in the cottage," Cheryl said. "I wish I knew what she likes."

"A variety pack, then," Kathy said. "A half dozen that are all different. We'll avoid nuts completely, in case of allergies, and I even have a couple options that are gluten- and dairy-free."

Cheryl agreed. "That sounds good. Yes, six fresh warm muffins, all different, to welcome Sugarcreek's newest resident."

Behind Cheryl, Doug grunted, and she turned.

He caught her eye. "Good luck."

"What do you mean?" Cheryl said.

"Feisty woman, tall, late thirties, a temper, bushy hair, driving a U-Haul towing a small Toyota?"

"I haven't met her yet." Of Doug's description, Cheryl could only attest to the fact that the person she was soon to meet was a woman.

Doug slurped some coffee. "If it's the same person I ran into a few minutes ago, brace yourself. She likes to take her half of the road out of the middle and will give you a string of reasons why it's none of your business if she does."

"But I'm taking muffins," Cheryl said brightly. And her adorable baby would help break the ice. Who knew what the truth of the encounter in the street might have been? Anyone who had ever moved understood how stressful moving day was, and Cheryl was fairly sure Jayla was arriving on her own.

"All set." Kathy handed Cheryl a container of half a dozen muffins.

Cheryl paid for the baked goods, arranged them in the gift basket so they would be both prominent and stable, made sure the baby was settled, and steered the stroller out the door. Outside, she waved at Esther Miller, her sister-in-law and employee at the Swiss Miss. Esther had been working there since before Cheryl's arrival. The shop still belonged to Cheryl's aunt, so she felt an obligation to maintain a presence and keep up-to-date with what was going on in the store. The truth was, though, Esther was fully capable of running the Swiss Miss. Especially since Rebecca's arrival eighteen months ago, Cheryl enjoyed the flexibility that Esther's competence and reliability gave her.

The four-block walk was familiar from the hundreds of times Cheryl had walked between the cottage and the Swiss Miss while living in the neighborhood before her marriage. Taking the steps stirred up a wave of wistfulness for her own early days in Sugarcreek. When she arrived, she knew her purpose. On the surface, she'd come to run her aunt's shop. Underneath, she needed a fresh start after a broken engagement. Aunt Mitzi hadn't said what brought Jayla Nuttall to Sugarcreek. Surely, she could have rented the cottage to someone already living in town. She could have put up a notice or spread the word, and someone would have known someone who needed a place. Instead, Mitzi chose Jayla and gave Cheryl instructions to make an effort.

Pushing a stroller with a toddler and a gift basket required more physical effort than just getting herself four blocks down the street. A woman fitting Doug's description was unhitching a flatbed trailer from the U-Haul with every indication that she knew exactly what she was doing. She'd already unchained and rolled a red Toyota off the trailer.

Small Toyota. Check.

Feisty. Check.

Tall. Check.

Bushy hair. Check.

U-Haul. Check.

The woman dropped the safety chains from the trailer hitch and looked up. "You're late." Irritation throbbed in her tone.

"Technically, I suppose," Cheryl said. "But just a couple of minutes."

"Late is late. I don't have all day."

Jayla disconnected some wires. Brake lights on the trailer, Cheryl guessed. Then Jayla stomped—there really was no more polite word for it—to the trailer tires and kicked at the stability wedges to check their worthiness.

Temper. Check.

"Welcome to Sugarcreek," Cheryl said. "Did you have any trouble finding your way?"

"It's the twenty-first century. I have a smartphone and GPS. There's no excuse for anyone to get lost."

"Sometimes these small towns…" Cheryl regretted starting a sentence she didn't know how to finish.

Jayla scalded her with a glare yet did not interrupt her own flow of movement to unhook the empty trailer and gain access to the truck's contents.

"I brought some things you might enjoy." Cheryl picked up the basket and held it toward Jayla. "Some items from some of the shops in town and coupons for other places. I put in some restaurants. You might need some easy meals until you get settled in."

Jayla pushed down on the trailer latch and turned the wheel to release the clamp.

"Are you hungry now?" Cheryl said. "The muffins from the Honey Bee Café are fresh, and they are the *best*. I should have thought to bring coffee. I'd be happy to go back and get some."

Jayla shook her head, her bushy black hair waving like a Don't Bother Me flag.

"It's a welcome basket," Cheryl said.

Jayla's brown eyes rolled. She finally came closer to Cheryl, making plain that her full height was a good nine inches taller than Cheryl's five-foot-two-inch frame. Her mass of hair, while bushy, nevertheless carried style Cheryl's own short red hair would never attain.

"Your aunt said you'd have the lease and the keys," Jayla said.

"Yes. Shall we go inside?" Cheryl would just leave the basket on the counter and be done with it. "I'll show you around and answer whatever questions you have."

"It can't be that complicated," Jayla said. "Light switches, a fuse box, appliances. All the usual features, right?"

"Yes, I guess so."

"I have your phone number and email," Jayla said. "I'll let you know if anything comes up."

Rebecca roused in the stroller, this time more than a mild protest. This cry was a demand to be lifted.

"Just a minute." Cheryl set the basket on the sidewalk and reached into the stroller. Perhaps the sight of the child would shift the mood. She turned her daughter toward Jayla. "This is Rebecca."

Jayla looked at Rebecca for about three seconds but said none of the pleasant things people usually say about a baby. No inquiries about her age or disposition. No admiration of her beauty, her big blue eyes, her winning smile, her plump cheeks. It was as if Rebecca were not even there, or at least that her presence was of no consequence.

"Keys?" Jayla said. "Lease?"

"Of course." Cheryl knew better than to put Rebecca down so soon after a "hold me" cry, so she fumbled with one arm on the rack beneath the stroller bed for the purse that held the lease and keys—and hopefully a pen. Under the circumstances, and given

Jayla's mood, to show up unprepared for the signing would provoke another eye roll and a series of curt remarks.

The lease was uncrumpled, and Cheryl found not one but two pens.

"Do you have someone to help you unload?" Cheryl pressed the lease against her own leg to sign it then handed it and a pen to Jayla. "I could probably make some calls."

"I'll be fine. I always manage on my own."

No one should have to speak that sentence.

Jayla signed the lease and handed it back to Cheryl.

Cheryl pulled a set of keys from a purse pocket. "Back door and front door," she said.

"Like I said, can't be that hard." Jayla turned, went up the walk, and let herself into the cottage.

Cheryl pushed out the sigh she'd been holding in since her first sight of Jayla Nuttall. If she paid her rent on time and didn't damage the cottage, that's all that mattered. Cheryl couldn't force her to be friends. Where had Aunt Mitzi even found this woman? Making an effort was one thing. This would be like moving a mountain.

Cheryl put the basket in the stroller and kept Rebecca in her arms as she pushed it back toward the Swiss Miss.

A Note from the Editors

We hope you enjoy Sugarcreek Amish Mysteries, created by the Books and Inspirational Media Division of Guideposts, a nonprofit organization that touches millions of lives every day through products and services that inspire, encourage, help you grow in your faith, and celebrate God's love in every aspect of your daily life.

Thank you for making a difference with your purchase of this book, which helps fund our many outreach programs to military personnel, prisons, hospitals, nursing homes, and educational institutions. To learn more, visit GuidepostsFoundation.org.

We also maintain many useful and uplifting online resources. Visit Guideposts.org to read true stories of hope and inspiration, access OurPrayer network, sign up for free newsletters, download free e-books, join our Facebook community, and follow our stimulating blogs.

To learn about other Guideposts publications, including the best-selling devotional *Daily Guideposts*, go to ShopGuideposts. org, call (800) 932-2145, or write to Guideposts, PO Box 5815, Harlan, Iowa 51593.

Find more inspiring fiction in these best-loved Guideposts series!

Secrets of Wayfarers Inn

Fall back in history with three retired schoolteachers who find themselves owners of an old warehouse-turned-inn that is filled with hidden passages, buried secrets and stunning surprises that will set them on a course to puzzling mysteries from the Underground Railroad.

Tearoom Mysteries Series

Mix one stately Victorian home, a charming lakeside town in Maine, and two adventurous cousins with a passion for tea and hospitality. Add a large scoop of intriguing mystery and sprinkle generously with faith, family, and friends, and you have the recipe for *Tearoom Mysteries*.

Mysteries of Martha's Vineyard

What does Priscilla Latham Grant, a Kansas farm girl know about hidden treasure and rising tides, maritime history and local isle lore? Not much—but to save her lighthouse and family reputation, she better learn quickly!

Mysteries of Silver Peak

Escape to the historic mining town of Silver Peak, Colorado, and discover how one woman's love of antiques helps her solve mysteries buried deep in the town's checkered past.

**To learn more about these books,
visit Guideposts.org/Shop**